FATTER, SLOWER, WORSER

FREAKS UNITED
OFFSIDE!

John Hickman

award

ISBN 978-1-78270-275-7

Text copyright © 2017 John Hickman
Cover illustration by Stephen Robertson
Football illustration by Loveandrock/Shutterstock.com
This edition copyright © Award Publications Limited

First published by Award Publications Limited 2018

Published by Award Publications Limited,
The Old Riding School, Welbeck,
Worksop, S80 3LR

18 1

Printed in the United Kingdom

For Abby, Brooke,
Finn and Siobhan

THE BIG QUESTION

'But how would we fit eleven players into a five-a-side team?' asked Beefy. He stared up at the ceiling, with his eyebrows right up on his forehead, concentrating really hard on the maths.

'We'd have to leave people out,' said Angelo. 'Wouldn't we?'

Seth stared at the poster on the Soccerdome noticeboard again.

Do you love football?
Are you under 16?
Are you ready for a challenge?
5-A-SIDE TOURNAMENT
May 23rd to May 24th
The winning team will meet
star striker Jesse Walters!

Jesse Walters was Seth's absolute favourite

player. He was only nineteen and he was already United's first choice striker. He was top scorer in the league and he'd been called up to the England squad. The pundits on the TV were already saying Walters would go on and be one of the all-time greats. He was pretty much everything Seth wanted to be. This chance was too good to be true. A chance to meet his hero. 'We have to enter,' he said.

Angelo stared hard at the tournament address details. 'Shell Bay... where even is that?' he asked. 'Sounds miles away.'

'So what?' said Seth. 'We can sort all that. Get a minibus or something.'

'And who'll drive us?' asked Angelo. 'Got your licence now, have you?'

Seth didn't care about all the obstacles in his way. The opportunity to meet Jesse Walters was too big not to try. And as much as he didn't want to admit it to himself, this was about more than just meeting his hero. Everything had started when Seth's horrible PE teacher, Mr Steele, had told Seth he wasn't good enough for the school team. He was 'too slow', Beefy was 'too fat' and Angelo was 'a liability'. They hadn't taken the knock-back lying down. No way. They'd started their own team. Now, Seth still dreamed of being a professional footballer. The ultimate dream – the dream of all dreams – was to play for United. He knew it was a long shot. That it would probably never happen. But if Seth set his mind to something, he really believed he could achieve things. He'd proved he had the determination. He'd got Freaks United up and running, hadn't he? If Jesse Walters could see him play, who knows what might happen? Maybe he could get a trial with United. How amazing would that be?

Seth realised there was someone else looking at the poster on the Soccerdome noticeboard. He looked a bit older than Jesse Walters. He was wearing a United tracksuit – the red and black one Seth had been banging on at his dad to get him. He was tall and athletic-looking with short, styled hair and chiselled cheekbones. He looked just like the movie star Will Smith.

'Looks good,' said the guy. 'You lot thinking of going?'

'Yeah,' Seth replied. 'Thinking about it.'

'You should, be awesome to go. And who knows, you could meet Jesse Walters. How sick would that be?'

Seth nodded. 'Proper sick.'

'Super sick,' Angelo added.

And Beefy just mumbled the word 'sick' to himself. He was staring at the guy in this really weird way, like he was a god or something.

'Where's Shell Bay?' asked Angelo. 'Sounds miles away.'

'Not far,' said the guy. 'Couple of hours, if that.'

'See,' said Seth, smugly. 'Not far.'

'I've just started teaching in a school nearby,' the guy told them. 'Well, I'm starting tomorrow. Might see if I can get a few kids together and take a team along myself.' He gave Seth and his mates a nod. 'Might see you there, boys.' Then he strolled away, his Nike backpack slung over his shoulder.

Angelo stared after him. 'Man, why can't we have a teacher like that?' he asked.

'I know,' Seth agreed. 'We get stuck with that old dinosaur, Steele. Did you see his United tracksuit?'

'It was sick,' said Beefy, who was still staring after the guy. 'D'you know what? I think he might've been the coolest man I've ever seen. He was really handsome wasn't he?'

Seth shot Angelo a little glance and raised his eyebrows.

'Since when do you say "sick"?' asked Angelo.

Beefy shrugged and made a little noise that sounded like 'I dunno'.

'So what d'you think?' asked Seth. 'You guys

up for it?'

Angelo smiled with half of his mouth. Beefy screwed his face up like he was sucking on a load of sour sweets.

Seth was feeling impatient. 'We doing this then, or what?' he asked. He held his hand out in front of the others, ready for them to put their hands in too.

'Who are you?' asked Angelo. 'Alan Block?'

Seth was getting impatient. 'Are you in or not?'

'I'm in, I'm in. Jeez,' Angelo replied. He put his hand on top of Seth's.

Seth looked at Beefy. 'Sick boy, you in? You might get to see that guy again!' Seth swallowed a giggle as Angelo burst out laughing.

'Shut up,' Beefy said, giving Seth's arm a little pinch. 'He was just really cool is all.'

'Beef, man, would you just put your hand in?' snapped Seth.

Beefy finally put his hand in too.

'Sweet.' Seth looked at them and nodded, pleased his mates were on board with the mission. 'Just that one problem – how *do* we fit eleven players into a five-a-side team?'

THE BEST OF FRIENDS

Once Seth's dad, Steve, had come out of the training rooms, Seth, Beefy and Angelo, sat on chairs at the side of the indoor pitch and watched him play a five-a-side with his mates. They weren't in a league or anything, it was just a bit of fun. Or at least that's what it was supposed to be. They did take it quite seriously, always shouting at each other.

There were brick walls all around the pitch, and the roof reminded Seth of a factory, with lots of metal framing and these big harsh lights. Seth loved indoor football. He loved the squeak of the trainers on the hard, shiny floor. It was always good to watch his dad play – especially with his mates.

Seth, Angelo and Beefy had been pretty much inseparable since they first made friends back in nursery school. Angelo was shorter than Seth, and skinnier, and his hair was braided in cornrows. Beefy had won them over instantly with a never-ending supply of sweets. He was like a less weird Willy Wonka. He was chunky, with freckles and short blonde hair. Seth was slim and taller than both his mates. He had short, mousy hair, nowhere near as cool as Angelo's cornrows. Seth always thought the three of them looked like an odd trio. They were a good starting point for Freaks United.

Seth watched as his dad got the ball under control. He twisted and turned, made himself a yard of space, and fired a hard shot, right into the bottom corner.

'GOAL, DAD!' shouted Seth.

'NICE ONE, BIG STEVE!' added Angelo.

'WOOHOO!' cheered Beefy, clapping.

Seth's dad was the best player on the team. But Seth would've probably thought that even if he wasn't. He definitely knew more about football than anyone else. That's why Seth asked him to help set up his own football team. Steve was the Freaks United coach. Seth thought back to how they had collected the team together – a Goth, a geek, a clown and people who were just plain weird, like Alan Block. They'd challenged Mr Steele's school team and played well, putting up a proper fight when no one – including themselves – had given them a chance. They might've lost, but everyone had such a laugh. They must've done something right, because the school's star player, Daniel Logan, asked if he could join them. Seth, Beefy and Angelo made him sweat for ages before they told him he was in.

All that happened just two months ago. It only seemed like two weeks. And now they were going to play proper games against proper teams. All because him and his mates didn't want to quit. It just goes to show, Seth thought, if there's something you love doing, you don't quit. No matter who tells you you're not good enough. Because you just never know.

But right now Seth was feeling weird about everything. He really wanted to play at that five-a-side tournament and meet Jesse Walters. This was big. But that question kept bouncing around in his mind. How would he fit eleven players into five places? Some of his mates were definitely going to miss out. Seth felt a twist in his belly.

He watched as his dad beat another man in a tackle and slotted the ball between the goalie's legs. He threw a fist in the air and shouted, 'GET IN!'

'MEGS!' shouted Angelo.

'WOOHOO!' cheered Beefy.

Seth nudged Beefy. 'Why d'you always do that – that "woohoo" thing?'

'It makes me sound excited,' Beefy told him.

'Makes you sound like a stupid little train,' said Angelo.

'Or some weird little ghost,' added Seth. 'Would you stop it?'

'I quite like it,' said Beefy. Then he kept on saying it – 'Woohoo woohoo woohoo!' over and over again, just to wind up Seth and Angelo.

Seth never thought he'd be so pleased to see Alan Block arrive on the scene with his podgy hamster cheeks, tiny eyes and ginger hair. He was wearing a T-shirt that said 'I'm my mum's favourite'.

'Hello, everyone,' said Alan Block. 'Was someone doing a ghost impression? I love ghosts.' Before anyone had the chance to say anything, he was shouting, 'HELLO, MR HART!' at Steve.

Steve looked over, nodded. 'ALL RIGHT, BIG AL!' he shouted back.

'YES, THANKS,' shouted Alan. 'I HAD FISH FINGER SANDWICHES FOR TEA, AND FOR PUDDING...'

Seth stuck his hand over Alan's mouth. 'He's playing a game man, he doesn't need to know.'

Alan stopped talking and Seth pulled his hand away.

'Guess what?' said Beefy. 'There was this really cool guy outside, I mean like one of the coolest guys I've ever met…'

'All right, Beefy,' said Seth. 'Give it a rest.'

'He was cool though,' Beefy protested.

'Was he cool?' asked Alan Block.

'So cool,' said Beefy.

'Go and marry him,' said Angelo.

'As if,' said Beefy. 'Did you see the poster outside, Al? About the…'

Seth gave him a kick in the shin, which shut Beefy up before he could go any further.

'Hey,' said Beefy. 'Not cool.'

'Alan doesn't need to know about that,' said Seth.

'Don't I?' asked Alan Block.

'No, mate,' Seth told him. 'You don't.'

'Oh,' said a disappointed Alan. 'It sounded like it might be cool.'

'Will you all stop saying "cool"?' snapped Seth. 'It's not cool.' He knew he was being harsh and overreacting. But he could feel that wrench in his stomach again. Fitting eleven players into a team of five was going to be *really* tough. And Alan Block probably wasn't going to make the cut.

A CHANGED MAN

It played on Seth's mind all weekend. He knew deep down that leaving behind half of the team to go to this tournament was wrong. It went against everything the Freaks stood for. Freaks United wasn't about winning. It was about taking part, getting involved, doing something you loved. Having fun. But the chance to meet Jesse Walters and maybe get a trial at United, that was all he really wanted. If there was even a sniff of a chance, he had to take it. Didn't he?

On Saturday night, Seth's Dad took him to Nandos before they went to watch the new Marvel movie. Under normal circumstances, Nandos was Seth's absolute favourite place to eat. He loved all the different hot sauces and being able to drink fizzy pop until he could feel it sloshing around inside him. But tonight he wasn't enjoying himself. He nibbled at his

17

chicken burger, his mind clearly somewhere else altogether.

'Everything all right?' asked Steve. 'You don't seem yourself.'

'I'm OK,' Seth replied.

'You know I'm not really one of those "if you want to talk about it" parents,' Steve told him. 'But if you want to talk about it...' He grinned at Seth like an idiot, and even though he was feeling awful inside, Seth forced a smile back.

'You sure you're OK?' asked Steve.

Seth's dad was easily over six foot and, at the last weigh in, he was over sixteen stone. His hair was short – number one – and he had a tanned face. He was a builder and sometimes, when he was doing work around the house, Seth even got an eyeful of builder's bum. Not what you want really. His dad had a weight bench in the garage. Seth sat and watched him do bench presses sometimes. He was ridiculously strong. And tough too. He was a black belt in Ju-jitsu. Seth remembered his dad offering to go down to the school and karate-chop Mr Steele after he'd been awful to Seth and his mates. If there was anyone Seth would ever talk to, it was his dad. While Jesse Walters was Seth's hero, his dad was up there too. His 'real life' hero. He looked up to his dad and listened to him, even though he pretended that he didn't sometimes.

Seth sighed. 'Might have a bit of a problem.'

'OK,' said Steve. 'I'm listening.'

'You know how you've always said I should follow my dreams and that?' asked Seth.

'I do, yeah,' Steve told him.

'Do you really mean it?' asked Seth.

'Of course. Hundred percent.'

Seth took another little bite from his burger – he knew he wasn't really telling his dad the full story. 'No matter what?'

'Is this about the Freaks?' asked Steve.

Seth exhaled a long, sad sigh through his nose. 'Hmm-mm.'

'I've told you,' said Steve, 'we'll have you in the league in no time. Just got a bit of paperwork to sort out.'

'I know.'

'Is that what's worrying you?' asked Steve. 'That it'll all go wrong?'

Seth shrugged. He thought about Beefy and made that same little 'I dunno' sound his mate always made.

'Honestly, mate, I'll get it sorted,' Steve told him. 'And I stand by what I said – you follow your dreams, you hear me?'

Seth nodded, feeling a little better.

'No matter what,' Steve added.

Seth's mind was made up. He was doing this. As hard as it was going to be, he was going to have to pick the best Freaks for the five-a-side team. And Alan Block definitely wasn't one of them.

It was Monday and Seth, Beefy and Angelo were hanging about in the school foyer, near the noticeboard where Seth had first put up the poster advertising Freaks United. Even now, he still felt his back go all cringey when he thought about Steele tearing the poster down and stuffing it in the bin. A part of Seth still wondered what would've happened if he'd let his dad come down to the school and unleash his karate skills on Mr Steele. He sort of wished he could go back and tells his dad, 'Yeah, go on, Dad, kick his butt!'

Seth's thoughts were interrupted by a strange little voice, which wasn't in his head. At least he hoped it wasn't. 'Whatcha doing?' said the little voice. It was all cartoony and cute, like something from a kids' TV programme.

Seth realised Alan Block was behind them. He was holding this little red monkey puppet thing, using his hand to make it talk. It had black buttons for eyes and was actually quite creepy.

A CHANGED MAN

'Erm, what you doing?' asked Seth.

'I asked you firsties,' said Alan Block, through the puppet. He was always up to something weird. If he wasn't videoing cats, he was practising his line dancing or building scarecrows. Playing with puppets must've been his new freaky fad. But somehow a day without Alan Block was pretty dull.

Seth frowned at Angelo and Beefy. 'Okaaay.'

'My name's Shlumpy,' said Alan's puppet. 'What's yours?'

'We've been though this, haven't we?' replied Seth. 'Being weird, doing weird things.'

'There's nothing weirds about Shlumpy,' said Alan's puppet.

'What's he called?' asked Angelo. 'Shlumby?'

Seth shook his head. 'Don't encourage him.'

'He's a cute little thing,' said Beefy. 'What is he?'

'Me's a monkey,' replied Alan's puppet.

Seth tilted his head back and groaned like a ghost.

'Ooh,' said Shlumpy. 'Me like that sound.'

'So you're a puppeteer now?' asked Seth, unimpressed with Alan Block's new venture.

'I got two puppet's ears,' Shlumpy told him, turning both sides of his head around to Seth. 'One here and one...'

Before Alan could finish his little routine, Seth wrestled the puppet away from his grasp and held his hand over the puppet's mouth. Alan made a 'mmmf mmmmf' sound as if Shlumpy were trying to talk. Beefy chuckled.

'Enough,' said Seth.

Alan sighed. 'OK.'

'I thought it was quite cute,' Beefy added.

'Me too,' said Angelo.

'Well I thought it was one of the most annoying things ever,' Seth told him. He gave the puppet back to Alan. 'What's wrong with you lot?' asked Seth, staring at his mates.

They all stared back, faces straight.

'Uh oh,' whispered Beefy, nodding across the foyer. 'Don't look now.'

They all looked instantly.

Seth watched as Mr Steele marched into school through the main entrance, with his shiny bald football head and bristly moustache. He was a short, stocky man with no neck, who looked a bit like a pit bull. He was wearing his trademark super-short shorts and a vintage City shirt from the 1980s. Seth's dad had a United one that was similar, which Seth had got him for Christmas. But Steele's was probably from the *actual* eighties. The PE teacher turned and smiled at Seth and the others, when he saw them. Seth thought that was *well* weird.

Steele never smiled.

Every time Seth saw Steele it all came back. Getting knocked back from the school team, and all the awful things Steele had said. Teachers were supposed to be nice. Fair. Friendly. They weren't supposed to be awful to kids. Mr Steele was a relic from a shoutier, bygone age. He probably wanted to bring back the cane.

Mr Steele marched on through the foyer, heading to the headmaster's office.

'Was it just me?' asked Seth. 'Or did he smile at us?'

'Maybe it was just wind,' said Beefy. 'You know, like a baby?'

Seth frowned. He had no idea what Beefy was on about.

'Hey,' whispered Angelo. 'I nearly forgot to tell you guys. I heard a few things,' he said. 'On the grapevine.'

'On the what now?' asked Seth.

'The grapevine,' Angelo repeated.

'On the grapevine,' said Alan Block. 'It means to learn of something by means of gossip or rumour, usually passed person-to-person by word of mouth, perhaps in a confidential manner among friends or colleagues

'Righto,' replied Seth. He nudged Angelo.

'Come on then, Ange, what you heard?'

Angelo glanced around, then beckoned his mates closer. The four of them gathered in a huddle. 'Got some top secret classified info,' he whispered.

'Are you an actual spy?' asked Alan Block, all excited and wide-eyed.

'Sort of.'

'Just tell us, man!' Seth hissed.

'Right, yeah,' said Angelo. 'Between you and me – between us – and you have to keep it on the DL, the down-low...'

'Just say it!' snapped Seth.

'I've heard there have been a few complaints,' said Angelo. He glanced around all over again, checking the coast was still clear.

Beefy glanced around too. He was clearly confused, wondering what Angelo's glancing around was all about.

'A few of the parents have had a go about Steele,' whispered Angelo. 'About him being a massive bully. How old-fashioned he is and that.'

'About time,' said Seth. 'I hope he gets booted out for good. Serves him right.'

Angelo nodded. 'So maybe that's why he's gone into Stephenson's office.'

Alan's eyes widened. 'Ummmm, do you

think he's getting *fired*?' he shouted.

Angelo elbowed Alan in the side. He didn't seem to notice. 'Shut it!'

'We should have a little sneak,' suggested Seth. 'Do some spying.'

'Can we?' asked Alan Block, giddy with excitement.

'Follow me,' whispered Angelo.

He scanned the foyer, looking like a weird ostrich with a luminous orange backpack and cornrows. Then he tiptoed towards the head's office, taking long slow steps, like some cartoon character.

Alan Block imitated Angelo precisely. The whole ostrich thing, the whole cartoony tippy-toe thing. And Beefy tried to the same, but his effort was much more half-hearted. Seth just stood there, watching his mates, wondering what crime he'd committed to be lumbered with such a bunch of morons.

Angelo pressed his ear against the dark wooden door of the head's office. Alan Block did the same. Beefy pressed the side of his face against the door. Seth just stood there, watching, as Alan slipped his puppet out of his satchel and pressed its little puppet face against the door too.

'Well?' asked Seth. 'Can you hear anything?'

'Shh,' said Angelo. 'We're listening.'

'Shh,' repeated Alan Block, in his little cutesy puppet voice.

Suddenly, the door opened. Angelo, Alan, Beefy and Shlumpy tumbled to the floor in a pile of school bags and blazers.

Mr Steele stood over the pile of kids, looking down on them. At first he just looked confused, his face all frowny. Seth thought he was going to go mad at them, but then Steele smiled – the widest and weirdest grin Seth had ever seen. 'Nice to see you,' said Mr Steele.

Angelo and Alan Block jumped to their feet. Beefy struggled to stand up quite as quickly as the other two, so they both grabbed an arm and pulled him up. The headmaster appeared in the doorway now, right behind Mr Steele. Mr Stephenson was a grey man. He wore a grey suit. Had grey hair. He even drove a grey car. 'Everything all right, Mr Steele?' he asked.

'Everything's hunky-dory,' replied the PE teacher.

'Right you are,' said Mr Stephenson. He gave Seth a curious look, then closed the door.

Mr Steele glanced behind him, checking the headmaster was gone. 'You lot spying again?' he asked. 'You like a bit of that don't you – spying?' But he didn't sound his usual obnoxious self. He sounded quite cheery, upbeat even.

Alan Block nodded, nervous and excitedly. Seth glared at him, shook his head. Alan's nod morphed into a shake. In fact, he shook his head so hard, Seth was sure it might come off.

'So have you been booted out for good?' Alan blurted.

The others gasped and Mr Steele scoffed, making this horrible snorting noise like a pig. 'Sacked? Me? You must be joking. I'm too well-liked round here.'

Seth stared at the teacher. There probably wasn't a person on the planet who liked Mr Steele. Not even his mum.

'Bet you'd have liked it if I had been though, heh?' Steele went on, staring at Seth so hard, Seth had to look away. 'Bet you'd have had a good old laugh at Mr Steele's expense, wouldn't you?' He narrowed his eyes on Seth, then stared at the boys. 'I'm here to stay. And I'll be seeing you all soon.' He grinned at them all over again – all wide and false – and he marched away as quickly as his tiny, tight shorts would allow.

The four lads just stood there, none of them saying a thing. Until Beefy piped up, 'Was that a threat?'

MR COTTON

That afternoon, Seth, Angelo and Beefy had PE. Seth had been dreading it all day, ever since their run-in with Mr Steele that morning. But he hated PE anyway. Seth still hadn't quite got the whole not-getting-picked-for-the-school-team thing out of his head. Even now, months on, he thought about it every time he stepped onto the school field. OK, it wasn't as bad as it had been, and having Freaks United helped massively. But he still felt embarrassed when he thought about how Steele had told him he was too slow. How he'd told Seth and his mates to give up football and take up knitting. Seth knew Steele was way out of line, but maybe Seth really wasn't good enough. Maybe his dreams of being a professional footballer, of playing for United – dreams so secret he'd never said them out loud to anyone – maybe they were a waste of time. Maybe Mr Steele was right and Seth would never make it.

Seth felt a dig in his ribs from Angelo beside him. 'Look,' he said.

'No way,' Beefy said excitedly.

Mr Steele, in his tight little shorts, was marching towards the group of boys, carrying a big holdall.

But there was someone else too.

A younger guy was also carrying cones. Seth knew he'd seen him somewhere before. But where?

Angelo nudged Seth. 'That's the guy, from the Soccerdome.'

It was the cool guy Seth had wished was his PE teacher, who'd encouraged them to give the five-a-side competition a go. Seth was excited and confused – what was he doing here? He wasn't as excited as Beefy though, who was staring at the new arrival like he had hearts floating out of his eyeballs and sailing away on the wind.

'Right you wonderful lot,' said Steele, dumping the holdall in front of the group. 'As you can see, I've got a bit of help today... not that I need it. Everyone, this is Mr Cotton – your new assistant PE teacher.'

Seth and the others grinned at Mr Cotton like he was a superhero, there to overthrow the diabolical dictator and usher in fun and happiness, smiles and joy and laughter and...

'Say hello then,' snapped Steele. 'Show the man some manners.'

All the boys said, 'Hello, Mr Cotton,' together, like six-year-olds. It reminded Seth of being in primary school.

'All right, boys,' said Mr Cotton. 'Nice to meet you all.' And he gave them a big smile. He had the whitest teeth. He definitely could've been a movie star. Seth had a new hero to add to his list, along with his dad and Jesse Walters. He was with Beefy on this one.

Mr Steele got the class performing various athletic events on the school field. They'd been throwing foam javelins, which Seth was pleased about. It was lucky they were foam. There's no way he'd have liked to have been around Angelo with a real javelin. Then they went on to the shot-put – a heavy metal ball the size of a grapefruit – which Alan Block lobbed approximately fifty-seven centimetres. Seth hated athletics. It was so boring, apart from watching Alan being super rubbish. All he wanted to do was play football.

Seth, Beefy and Angelo were queuing up to take their turn when Mr Cotton jogged over.

'All right, lads,' he said. 'Where do I know you lot from?'

'We saw you at the Soccerdome,' replied Seth.

'Last Friday.'

'Oh yeah. You were gonna enter the five-a-side competition – how's it going?'

'We're still thinking about it,' Seth told him.

'What's to think about?' asked Mr Cotton. 'Just do it. You'll be great.'

'YOU'RE UP, CARTER!' shouted Mr Steele.

Angelo grabbed a shot-put from the grass. 'It's pretty heavy innit?'

'Push from the feet,' Mr Cotton told him. 'Nothing to it.'

Encouraged by the new teacher's words, Angelo spun around and around... and around a bit more. Seth was getting dizzy just watching him.

'THROW IT, THEN!' bellowed Steele.

And Angelo threw it.

Right at Mr Steele.

It was an epic throw.

The heavy metal ball whacked Steele right in his tight little shorts.

Steele winced and doubled over.

'Ouch,' whispered Mr Cotton.

'Sorry,' Angelo called, weakly.

Seth's willpower evaporated and he burst out laughing. Even Mr Cotton couldn't stop himself from smiling.

Mr Steele looked up and saw them all wetting

themselves laughing. His red face went even redder. He looked like he was about to explode. But he didn't explode or shout out. Suddenly, he seemed able to bury his rage. He just laughed – a weird little laugh. 'Ha ha... it's fine.'

Seth was pretty sure he was forcing his words through gritted teeth. But this wasn't like Mr Steele at all? What was he up to?

BIG DECISIONS

That afternoon during break, Seth, Angelo and Beefy sat on the grass verge that ran around the concrete yard and watched the other kids in their year kick a ball around.

'Right then,' said Seth. 'Who we taking with us to this five-a-side tournament? We can only take six players, a team and one sub. There's already twice that playing for Freaks.'

There was a silence.

Beefy shook his head. 'Doesn't feel right,' he said. 'Leaving people out.'

No one needed to tell Seth it didn't feel right. He'd agonised over the whole thing all weekend. 'Don't you wanna meet Jesse Walters?' asked Seth. 'Because if you don't, we can just forget the whole thing.'

'It's not that,' Beefy replied. 'Course I wanna meet Jesse Walters. It's just...'

'Just what?'

'The whole point of Freaks was so that everyone could play,' Beefy told him. 'No one got left out.'

'I know,' said Seth. 'But it's just a weekend, isn't it? It's not forever. Freaks will still be here when we come back.'

'That's true,' added Angelo. 'It *is* just a weekend.'

'We just have to make sure the ones that don't get in don't find out,' Seth told him. 'Then there's no problem.'

Beefy sighed a big old sigh and stared at Seth. 'What if they do find out?'

'We'll make sure they don't.'

'We'd feel like rubbish if it was us that was left out,' said Beefy.

'If you don't wanna come, I can find other players,' Seth told him. He knew he was being mean as soon as the words came out of his mouth.

'I'm in,' said Angelo.

'Yeah?' asked Seth.

'Yeah,' replied Angelo. 'Like you said, Freaks will still be here. It's just a little trip away.'

'Beef?' asked Seth. 'What you saying?'

Beefy stared at Seth, then Angelo, then back at Seth. 'Go on then.'

'Good,' said Seth. 'You don't half make a meal

34

of things, don't you?'

'Meal of things,' said Angelo, snickering.

'That's not funny,' moaned Beefy as he stuffed three cheese puffs into his mouth.

'So how we gonna pick the other three players?' asked Beefy.

'There's not much choice,' Seth told him. 'If we want to win – and there's no other reason for us to be going unless we do – then we need to pick the best players.'

'We could take two teams,' suggested Beefy. 'Like an A and a B team?'

'Ooh,' said Angelo. 'That's a good idea.'

Seth had even thought about this too. 'But then only one of us could win. How rubbish would that be for the team that didn't?' There was another point Seth didn't mention. What would happen if a Freaks B team beat his five-a-side team and won the tournament? That would be the absolute worst. Losing to his mates. He wasn't sure he could deal with that in a sportsmanly way. He'd hate them for it. Who knows what something like that could do to Freaks United when they all got home?

'That would be rubbish,' agreed Angelo.

'But we don't care about winning,' Beefy told him. 'That's the Freaks United motto.'

'Actually, yeah,' said Angelo. 'Good point.'

'It's not though is it,' said Seth. 'It's actually "fatter, slower, worser".'

'Same thing,' replied Beefy.

'Surely we want to win this, though,' said Seth. 'How else are we gonna meet Jesse Walters?'

'He's got you there,' added Angelo.

'Look, don't think I haven't thought about this, because I have,' Seth told him. 'From every way you can think. Over and over until I wanted to bash my head against a wall. I mean, I was at the cinema with my dad the other day and all I could think about was who we'd be leaving at home.'

Beefy sighed again. 'In that case, we're probably gonna have to take Logan.'

Seth nodded. Out of all the Freaks, Logan was the best player. Unfortunately, he was Seth's least favourite Freak of all. Logan really thought he was something special. You could just tell how he reckoned every girl in school fancied him, walking around stinking of aftershave. He covered himself in so much of the stuff, it made Seth's eyes water.

'Laura too,' added Angelo.

Seth nodded in agreement. Laura was Alan's sister and she was an *awesome* player. 'Who else?' he asked. 'Who's the sixth player?'

'I know who I'd like to come the most,' said

Angelo.

Seth sighed. 'Me too.'

'Alan Block,' said Beefy.

'Thing is,' Seth replied. 'As funny as Alan Block is...'

'He's really funny though, Seth,' Angelo said firmly.

'I know and I don't even care that he's super weird,' Seth pointed out.

'He could be like a mascot,' said Angelo. 'With that little puppet thing. What was it Stumpy?'

'Shlumpsty, I think,' Beefy replied.

'But he's not great at footie, though, is he?' asked Seth. 'When he first turned up at trials we thought he was the world's worst player.'

'He's been getting better,' said Beefy.

'True, but we can't take everyone. We'll have to leave out loads of people – John, Curtis, Alex, Ryo...'

Just then, Seth spotted something strange. Mr Steele was peeping out from behind the gym wall. Seth frowned, nudged Beefy. 'Is he spying on us?' he whispered.

Beefy and Angelo spotted Steele too, standing there, peeping, all awkward in his little shorts. As soon as Steele spotted them spotting him, he blew the silver whistle that hung round his neck.

'YOU BOYS,' he shouted. 'SHOULDN'T YOU BE IN CLASS?'

'It's breaktime,' said Angelo.

'CLASSES, NOW!' he yelled.

The lads grabbed their things and jogged away.

As Seth hurried inside the school building, an idea came into his head. 'You don't think he heard us, do you?' he asked.

GETTING THE NEW TEAM TOGETHER

On Wednesday night, Seth and the others were at a Freaks United training session, over on Barrowby field, where they'd trained ever since they first started the team. Everyone was there: Seth, Beefy, Angelo and Alan Block, Laura, Logan, Big Sam, Tall John, Curtis, Ryo, Alex and Laura's best mate, Brooke – another new recruit, who was a pretty good player too. The only player who hadn't stuck around from the beginning was Jordan McGrath. Seth had been a bit gutted that Jordan had lost interest after the game against the school team, but he was also relieved. Jordan genuinely scared him and he was never quite sure what he would do next. So basically Logan had replaced him, and although Seth liked Logan a lot less, at least he was a bit more predictable.

Seth could still remember the first training session, when Curtis rocked up in his loafers, and Alex was wearing his big steel toe-capped Goth boots. Not only had they got them all wearing the right kind of footwear, but they could all play a bit of football now too. Mostly. Standing there, looking at everyone – from the super-tall John to the super-small Curtis – Seth was proud of what they'd achieved. That feeling only made what he was planning all the worse.

Once Steve had made them all do their stretches and warm-up exercises – which consisted of far too many squats and star jumps – he sorted them into two teams. When they'd first started up, Seth hated being put with Alan Block – he was so bad at football, it was ridiculous. He'd been literally scared of the ball. But now Alan wasn't scared of footballs. He quite liked them. So much so, he'd drawn a face on one and named it Peter, for no reason whatsoever. And Seth quite liked playing with him. In fact, he didn't mind who he was put with – everyone was cool. That's why he felt awful about this whole five-a-side thing. Everyone *was* cool. No one deserved to be left behind. But what could he do?

'Right, then,' said Steve. He booted the ball in the air and took his usual spot in goal.

Everything started as a nice, fun, relaxed knock-about. Until Beefy took a shot. There was a loud bang and everyone jumped. Alan Block even jumped down to the ground. 'GET DOWN!' he shouted in this weird American army accent.

But they weren't under attack. Beefy had toe-poked the ball so hard, it had burst. The ball had actually popped.

When everyone realised what had happened, they all exploded with laughter.

'Donkey,' jeered Seth, and made this 'eeyore' noise. The others joined in, making donkey noises at Beefy: 'EEYORE!', 'HEE-HAW!' Alan Block was making a chomping noise, grabbing clumps of grass from the ground and stuffing them in his mouth.

Steve gestured to Beefy empty-handed. 'They've got a point, mate,' he said, with this big grin.

Beefy frowned, he knew exactly what was coming. Steve rummaged around in his holdall and pulled out a donkey mask and a pair of shorts.

'Here you go, sunshine,' said Steve, handing the little outfit to Beefy.

'Ahh, man,' moaned Beefy, totally gutted. He pulled on the furry, grey donkey mask, with big ears and big teeth. He then pulled on the shorts over his tracksuit pants. They had a plastic bum cheeks sewn into them. The 'donkey suit' was the forfeit given to any player who did something particularly daft or clumsy. Popping a football with an almighty toe-poke was both, pretty much. It was all a bit of fun, and all the players loved it, giving Beefy stick, which he took on the chin.

'That's a lovely bottom you've got there, Mr Donkey,' said Alan Block, still chewing on grass himself. Everyone laughed.

After training, Seth, Angelo and Beefy went over to Logan and Laura while the others were changing their shoes and leaving the park. Logan was sorting out his boy-band hair and checking his pouty face, using his phone as a mirror. Laura was just standing there, watching him, shaking her head in disbelief. She was taller than Seth and had long, dark hair and big brown eyes like something out of a Japanese cartoon. Seth and his mates had all had a thing for Laura when they'd first met her. Not any more, though – she'd been dating Jordan McGrath, ex-Freak and the hardest kid in their year, for a couple of months. Seth didn't imagine Jordan would take kindly to anyone fancying his girlfriend, so he just forced himself to stop fancying Laura. It'd been quite hard at first, but he made himself imagine her with loads of boils and frizzy green hair and a long, crooked nose every time he saw her. It seemed to be doing the job.

Seth glanced about and made sure no one else was listening. 'How d'you two fancy meeting Jesse Walters?' Seth asked Laura and Logan.

'*The* Jesse Walters?' asked Logan.

'Yeah,' said Seth, looking around uncomfortably. 'Not so loud.'

'It's top secret,' added Angelo.

'What you lot on about?' asked Laura.

'There's a tournament,' Seth told her.

'Five-a-side,' added Beefy.

'Five-a-side,' repeated Seth. 'The winning team gets to meet Jesse Walters.'

'No way,' said Logan. 'Are we going?'

'Hopefully,' Seth replied. 'Thing is, you can't tell any of the others.'

'How come?' asked Laura.

'It's only five-a-side,' Seth told her.

'Five-a-side,' repeated Angelo, pointing at each of them and counting out loud. 'One... two... three...'

'So, not everyone can come,' added Seth.

'I'm in,' Logan told him. 'Fully, all day long.'

Seth wasn't surprised Logan was up for it. He wouldn't care much for the Freaks who'd be left behind if it meant he'd be heading for glory.

'OK,' said Laura. 'Jesse Walters is pretty hot.'

'So you'll keep it to yourself?' Seth asked.

'Yeah, man,' Logan replied and nodded. 'No worries.'

'Laura?' asked Seth. 'What about you?'

'I can't leave Alan,' said Laura. 'He's my little bro.'

Seth sighed, and stared at Beefy and Angelo. Then he looked over at Alan Block, who was now showing Steve his little red monkey puppet while Steve looked on, bemused.

OPERATION STEVE

'You won't say anything, then, Alan?' Seth was looking at Alan Block intently. 'It'll all be fine when we get back – the team will be together again. But you've got to keep it a secret. OK?'

Seth saw Alan's small blue eyes flash with excitement. He'd used the right buzzword. Secrets, plans and spying. Anything remotely connected to any of those things would get the job done.

Alan Block put his hand on Seth's shoulder. 'I absolutely swear I'll keep this top secret. There's no one capable of keeping a top secret top secret better than me.'

Seth looked at him. 'We're not messing about here.'

Alan nodded and held his fist out to Seth. 'Sure, bro.'

Seth just stared at him like he was from another planet.

After training, Seth and his dad headed home, along with Beefy and Angelo. Seth had told his dad that he and his mates were going to play video games, but deep down, he had another plan – he was going to convince Steve to take them to the five-a-side tournament.

When they got home, Steve ran himself a deep bath. 'Just off to soak my weary old bones,' he said. He paused and Seth imagined his dad was waiting for someone to tell him he wasn't old at all. But they didn't.

The lads waited until he was upstairs and out of earshot before they spoke.

'We ready, then?' asked Seth.

'Ready for what?' asked Beefy.

'Hmm, what have we been on about all day?'

Beefy just stared at him, blankly.

'Getting my dad to take us to the tournament?' Seth told him.

'Oh right, yeah,' Beefy replied. 'I'm tired. My brain's all sleepy.'

'All dead more like,' said Angelo, and Beefy gave him a playful whack on the arm.

Seth pulled Angelo up before he got into a play-fight with Beef. 'Come on then, let's get this done.'

'Isn't he in the bath, though?' asked Beefy.

'Exactly,' Seth told him. 'He'll say anything to

get rid of us!'

'Can we call it "Operation Steve"?' asked Angelo.

'If we have to.' Seth hurried out of the room and up the stairs. He knocked on the bathroom door. 'Daaad,' he said, stretching the word out the way he always did when he wanted something.

'Operation Steve is in full effect,' whispered Angelo, and Seth frowned at him.

'Uh oh,' replied Steve from the other side of the bathroom door. 'I know that voice.'

Angelo grasped the door handle and before they knew it the boys were all in the bathroom staring at Steve relaxing in the tub. Luckily, as always, his dad had used lots of bubble bath.

'Me and the lads were wondering,' said Seth, 'whether you'd do something really nice for us.'

'Really awesome,' added Angelo.

'Really sick,' Beefy added too.

'Ummm lads, can it wait a bit? I'm sort of in the bath.'

'You're not sort of in the bath, are you?' said Seth.

'Right,' said Steve. 'I'm *in* the bath.'

'And we won't keep you,' Seth told him.

'Come on, then,' said Steve. 'Hurry up, what d'you want?'

'So there's this five-a-side tournament coming

up,' Seth pointed out.

'OK, right.'

'And we were wondering,' Seth went on. 'Me and the lads, the boys...'

'You want me to take you?' asked Steve.

'Would you?'

'Yeah, Big Steve, would you?' added Angelo.

'Please, Big Steve,' said Beefy.

'Where is it?' asked Steve.

'It's, erm... just a coupla hours,' Seth told him.

'Right,' said Steve, sounding more and more suspicious. 'And how long will we be there?'

'Not long,' Seth told him.

'How long?' asked Steve.

'Just, erm... a coupla days,' Seth replied. 'May the 23rd and 24th.' He scrunched himself up, his face, his body, his hands, waiting for his dad's reaction.

Then it came. The answer Seth and his mates didn't want to hear: 'No can do, boys, sorry,' said Steve.

'Why not, though?' moaned Seth.

'I've got loads on at work at the minute,' Steve told him. 'Too much to go gallivanting off for a couple of days.'

'But, Daaad,' said Seth, the same way he did whenever he was trying to get his dad to change his mind about something.

OPERATION STEVE

'I'm sorry, boys, there's nothing I can do.'

'You work too much,' said Angelo. 'You could do with a holiday.'

'Doesn't really sound like much of a holiday to me,' Steve pointed out.

'It will be,' Seth told him. 'It's right by the coast. You could go sunbathing while we play the games and that.'

'Sunbathing?' asked Steve. 'Me?'

'Or get an ice cream or something,' said Angelo.

'Or go on a donkey ride,' added Beefy.

'As brilliant as all that sounds, it's still a no.'

Seth stared at his mates, totally gutted. They were so close. So close. They had the players — everyone had agreed to keep things quiet — and they were on their way to the tournament. On their way to meeting Jesse Walters.

'The winner gets to meet Jesse Walters,' Seth told him, playing his ace card.

'What, from United?' asked Steve.

'Yeah, Dad, from United.'

Steve was staring down at the bubbles in the tub. He looked like he was thinking hard. He sighed and looked at them all. 'Sorry, boys,' Steve told them. 'I really am.'

But Seth already had a plan.

WORK COMMITMENTS

The lads had to get to that tournament: it was their destiny. They couldn't just give up. Seth hadn't allowed it when Mr Steele had knocked them back for the school team, and he wouldn't have it now. So that Saturday, Seth, Angelo, and Beefy rocked up at Steve's worksite, all of them wearing old clothes and hi-vis vests they'd grabbed from Seth's garage.

Seth led his mates through a gate, and onto a patch of land. It'd been an old factory six months ago, but that was long gone now and instead there was scaffolding everywhere and new houses being built. There were a few blokes in hard hats and hi-vis vests working and a JCB digging up the ground. Seth could hear men shouting, hammering and drilling, and a radio playing somewhere on the site.

Seth and his mates hurried over to one of the builders who was turning cement in a big mixer.

WORK COMMITMENTS

'Excuse me,' said Seth. 'I'm looking for my dad – Steve Hart?'

The man laughed slightly at the sight of Seth and his mates in their hi-vis vests, looking like kids dressed as builders for a fancy dress party. 'Didn't realise it was bring your kids to work day,' he said.

Seth wasn't in the mood for funny little conversations. He was on a mission. 'Do you know where my dad is?' he asked again.

'Yeah yeah, OK,' said the man. Then he shouted out, 'STEVO!'

'WHAT-O?' Steve shouted back.

'HERE A MINUTE,' yelled the man, looking back over his shoulder.

After a moment, Steve appeared from inside a half-built house. When he saw Seth, Angelo and Beefy, all in their little builders costumes, he smirked. 'What's going on?' he asked.

'Looks like you've got a fan club,' the man told him.

'This is my son – Seth,' said Steve. 'And his mates – Angelo and Beefy.'

'Oh right – the footballers?' asked the man.

'This is them.'

'Your old man's always banging on about you lot,' said the man. 'How proud he is of you all.'

Seth smiled, feeling pretty proud too. He

always knew his dad said nice things to him, but it was good to hear he said nice things about him to other people too.

'So what you all doing?' asked Steve.

'We've come to give you a hand, Big Steve,' said Angelo.

'Steve-O,' added Beefy.

'Big Stevo,' repeated Angelo.

'Hand with what?' asked a smiling Steve.

'Your work,' said Seth. 'We thought, if we helped out, you might get done quicker. That way you'd have some free time.'

'This to do with that tournament you were banging on about?'

'We'll do whatever we can,' said Seth, full of enthusiasm. 'We'll lay bricks, shovel stuff...'

'We're good at shovelling stuff,' added Angelo.

'Mostly horse poo,' Beefy pointed out, and Steve's workmate laughed.

'You're not gonna let it go, are you?' asked Steve.

Seth, Beefy and Angelo all smiled and shook their heads.

'What's all this, then?' asked the other builder. 'I'm Lee by the way.'

'All right, Lee,' said Seth, sensing he might have an ally.

'They want me to take them to this five-a-side

tournament,' Steve told him. 'But I've told them how much we've got on here.'

'Don't be such a misery,' said Lee. 'Take the lads to their tournament.'

Steve sighed. 'Come on, you know what Gary's been like lately.'

'How long is it?' asked Lee.

'Just a couple of days,' Seth told him.

'That all?' asked Lee. 'GARY, MATE,' he shouted. 'YOU GOT A MINUTE?'

After a moment, another man came over. He was older than Steve and Lee, and had a big belly and a thick beard like a pirate. 'Didn't realise we had new starters,' said Gary, smiling, when he saw Seth and his mates.

Seth shook his head. Did all builders make rubbish jokes when they first saw you?

'Steve's all right to have a couple of days off, isn't he,' said Lee. 'Take these lot to a five-a-side tournament.'

'Oh right, are these the Freaks United lads?' asked Gary.

'This is them,' Steve told him. 'The one and onlies.'

'Your dad's told us all 'bout your team,' said Gary. 'Got me to sponsor your shirts.'

'Thanks for that,' replied Seth. 'They're really cool.'

'Proper sick,' added Beefy.

'Beefy, man,' snapped Seth. 'Shush.'

'When you thinking?' asked Gary.

'In a couple of weeks,' Seth told him.

'We have got a lot on at the minute,' Gary pointed out. 'But if you can give us a hand then that'd free your dad up a bit,' Gary joked, winking at Steve and Lee.

'We can help out,' Seth told him.

'We can do whatever,' added Angelo.

'Shovelling, carrying things,' said Beefy.

'They've got experience,' said Lee. 'They've been telling us all about it.'

'You OK with them doing a few jobs, Steve?' asked Gary.

'Hey, if they wanna do a few jobs, they can do a few jobs.'

Once Gary had made sure Seth and mates were wearing all the right safety gear – proper hard hats – he led the lads over to a huge pile of rubble.

'Hope you've got strong backs,' he said. 'This lot'll take some shifting.'

Seth swallowed. 'All of it?'

'I'm afraid so,' replied Gary.

Seth had been here before, working for something he believed in. And he believed in this tournament. He wasn't afraid of a bit of graft. So he rolled up his sleeves. 'Come on, let's get shovelling.'

The lads worked away for ages, building up a proper sweat. It was hard work, but at least it didn't stink as bad as the pile of horse poo Big Sam and his grandad had got them shifting at the allotment in return for Sam joining the Freaks.

Steve came over to see what they were up to. 'How we getting on, then?' he asked.

'Not too bad,' said Seth.

'Not had enough yet?'

'We can go for days,' Angelo told him.

'Speak for yourself,' said Beefy, huffing and puffing away.

Steve laughed and shook his head. 'You lot make me laugh.'

'Does that mean you'll take us?' asked Seth.

'I dunno,' said Steve.

'Pleeease, Dad.'

'Please, Big Stevo,' added Angelo.

'Pleeease…'

'OK, OK,' said Steve, before Beefy said his bit. 'I'll take you.'

'No way,' said Seth. 'For real?'

'For real,' Steve told him.

Buzzing, Seth and Angelo and Beefy all

hugged Steve.

'Thanks, Dad, you're the best.'

'I know I am,' said Steve. 'Now, just one thing I want cleared up. It's five-a-side right?'

Seth nodded. 'Hmm-mm.'

'So how's that gonna work?' asked Steve. 'Two teams or...'

'We've already spoken with everyone,' Seth told him. 'We've, err, we've got it all sorted. Quite a few couldn't make it, and some weren't really up for it.'

'Yeah?' asked Steve.

'Yeah,' Seth replied. 'Sam has stuff to do at his grandad's shop, and John has homework, like always.'

'Ryo is practising clown stuff,' added Angelo.

'And Curtis is playing his games,' Beefy told him. 'With the little models and that. He's got Warhammer commitments.'

'Right,' said Steve. 'Just the one team, then?'

'Just the one team,' Seth repeated.

'And it's all squared?'

'All squared.'

'Because the whole point of Freaks—'

Seth interrupted his dad. 'No one's getting left out,' he lied.

THE NEW TEAM

'I spy with my little eye,' said Alan Block. 'Something beginning with…'

'No one wants to play I Spy,' Seth told him.

Seth, Angelo, Beefy, Alan, Laura and Logan were sat in the back of the minibus, while Steve sat up front, driving. All the way to Shell Bay, Alan had been trying to get the others playing games: I Spy, Twenty Questions and something called Super Cat Friends, which Seth was sure Alan had made up. No one was really listening. Logan was just staring at his own reflection in the window, tweaking his hair constantly. He couldn't help himself. Logan loved to look at himself whenever he got the chance – shop windows, car windows, windows in houses. Any sort of reflective surface would do the trick.

All the way there, Seth had just wanted some peace and quiet. He still felt awful for what he'd done. More awful in fact, because he was actually doing it. He was actually leaving half the Freaks out of something. None of them had found out, thankfully. He'd pulled off the deception.

He'd had to be super sneaky to make sure his dad hadn't discovered he'd lied about the others not wanting to go along to the tournament. He'd cancelled the last training session, telling all his teammates that Steve was sick, and telling his dad that there was a bug going around the school and all his teammates were poorly. That way he'd avoided any unnecessary conversations Steve might've had with Sam or John or Curtis about them being too busy for the five-a-side tournament. It was sly and underhand, and Seth hated doing it, but he had to, if he was going to meet Jesse Walters.

The weekend of the tournament had rolled around quickly. It was just like the time the Freaks faced off against the school team. Seth tried not to think about the tournament, about his big chance to meet Jesse Walters, but it had been on his mind all the while. And then, before he knew it, they were all in a little minibus that Steve had hired for the trip. Him and the others all headed to the coast for the five-a-side tournament.

Eventually they pulled into the car park of a big,

old-fashioned looking hotel. It was a horrible dirty yellow colour and it had dark red columns and window frames. Seth wasn't massively experienced when it came to hotels, but this one didn't look the best. In fact, it looked like the sort of place they'd use in horror films. The more Seth stared at it, the more it gave him the creeps. Still, though, he couldn't wait to get out of the minibus and away from Alan Block and his attempts to have 'fun'.

Seth was glad to stretch his legs and get some fresh air. It was lovely and sunny. Perfect weather for a weekend at the coast. The sky was a brilliant bright blue and there wasn't a cloud in sight.

Steve inhaled a long breath. 'Smell that sea air.'

'What is this place?' asked Laura.

'It's a hotel,' said Steve, sarcastically.

'Is it?' asked Laura, even more sarcastically.

'It was cheap and it's all there was,' Steve told her. 'So it'll have to do.'

Inside, the place was even worse. There was no one around and it looked like it hadn't been decorated since the beginning of time. The carpets were all flowery and swirly. They made Seth dizzy just from staring at them.

'I think you should wear the donkey suit next

time, Big Stevo,' said Angelo. 'State of this place.'

'I can drive you all back, if you want?' Steve suggested.

'I like it,' said Alan, staring around the reception area.

'See, at least someone appreciates my hard work,' said Steve.

'There's probably ghosts here,' added Alan. 'There's usually ghosts in places where people die.'

Seth and the others burst out laughing, all except Beefy. He looked genuinely scared by the prospect of staying somewhere haunted.

Everyone dumped their gear in their little musty and mouldy rooms and Seth and the others waited for Logan to unpack his toiletries. Seth couldn't believe how much stuff Logan had. There were so many sprays and creams and hair products, it was like he'd brought an entire salon with him.

'Right,' said Steve, once everyone had gathered outside the creepy hotel. 'We'll get you lot fed and watered, *then* you can check out the arcades or whatever. We'll meet back here for eight, you all got that?'

'Yes, Steeeve,' Seth and his mates moaned together.

THE NEW TEAM

Two cars pulled into the car park. A little red car and an old blue car, which looked big and expensive, like something out of a museum.

'At least there are other humans staying here,' said Laura and everyone laughed.

The door of the big blue car opened and out stepped a black leather cowboy boot.

Whoever was climbing out was wearing blue denim jeans and a blue denim jacket. He also had on shades like pilots wear.

Then Seth realised he recognised the person climbing out of the car.

It was Mr Steele.

Seth gasped. He actually gasped. His breathing, his heart, his everything stopped completely. Seth was shocked to see the PE teacher. Especially out of his trademark super-short shorts. He probably thought he looked the business in his denim outfit and his shades. But he really didn't. He looked like a joke. A small, red-haired lady got out of the passenger side of Steele's car. She was wearing really bright clothes – a yellow shirt, bright blue jeans, pink trainers. She had this really trendy haircut, long on one side and short on the other, and she had a sparkly stud in her nose.

'Is that Steele?' asked Angelo.

'And is that his wife?' asked Logan.

'What's she doing with someone like him?' asked Laura.

Then things got much, *much* worse.

Mr Cotton got out of the red car and a bunch of kids piled out of both cars – Big Sam, Tall John, Ryo, Alex, Little Curtis and Laura's best mate, Brooke.

Seth's stomach sank. This was his worst nightmare.

THE OLD TEAM

They stood there, Mr Steele and the other Freaks, all staring at Seth, Beefy, Angelo and the others. No one said a word for what seemed like forever.

'Awkward,' whispered Laura.

That was one word for it, thought Seth.

'This is like that film, isn't it,' said Alan Block. 'With Iron Man and Captain America, the one where they hate each other and have that big fight with airplanes?'

Seth knew the film Alan was talking about, and while this probably wouldn't end in a civil war, it would definitely put a massive crack right through the middle of Freaks United.

Steve scratched his neck awkwardly. 'What's going on? What's the team doing with *him*?'

Seth stared at his other teammates. Their faces were blank. From Tall John to Small Curtis. Sam, Ryo, all of them. The only one who was sort of smiling was Alex, standing there in his dark make-up and big steel toe-capped boots. Seth wished the concrete car park below him would cave in. He wished he could fall and fall into the darkness.

'They're with me,' Steele told him, 'because they felt left out. When they found out about this five-a-side tournament and how only "the best" Freaks had been invited along, well I'm sure you can imagine...'

Steve glared at Seth. 'Is this true?'

Seth didn't know what to say, so he just stared down at the grey concrete beneath his feet.

'You see, Mr Hart,' Steele went on. 'I'm all about inclusion and making sure everyone gets a fair chance – I couldn't leave these wonderful young people sad and upset now, could I? I couldn't very well do nothing.'

Seth suddenly realised what Mr Steele had done. He'd spied on them and found out what Seth had been planning. He'd worked out the ultimate payback for Freaks embarrassing his school team. Seth swallowed hard. He'd handed Steele his revenge on a plate.

'I can see exactly what you're doing,' said Steve.

'I'm not sure I know what you mean,' Mr Steele replied, pretending to be all innocent.

'No, I'll bet,' said Steve. 'How old are you exactly?'

Steele looked around, all squirmy and embarrassed. 'I don't see—'

'Too old to be pulling stunts like this.'

'And wearing that outfit,' muttered Laura.

Angelo and Beefy laughed.

'You've got me all wrong,' Steele told him. 'You see, you and your team here – well, when it was a team at least – you taught me I was too harsh. Too strict. You showed me the error of my ways.'

Mr Cotton smiled awkwardly at Seth and his mates, like he wanted to say something and wasn't sure what. Seth looked away, red-faced.

'But I'm a changed man now,' Steele went on. 'A modern man. I've got myself an electronic tablet, I've taken up meditation. I just want young people to have fun. Learn. Live their lives. *That's* what I'm doing.'

Seth looked at Angelo and Beefy. Was he telling the truth? He couldn't be, could he? Steele was from the old school. The 'treat 'em mean' team. Seth wasn't sure whether Steele was trying to get back at him and his dad, and ruin Freaks for good, or whether he really just wanted to help. Could he be for real?

'So if you'll excuse us,' said Steele. 'I need to

get this lot settled in and ready for the tournament.' With that, he led Mr Cotton, his bright little red-haired wife and the other half of Freaks United into the rundown hotel. Seth could barely look at Sam and John and the others as they passed him.

'Seth,' snapped Steve. 'A word.'

Once Steve had given Seth a proper telling off for lying to him, Seth, Beefy, Angelo and the others trudged along the beach, eating trays of chips as seawater washed onto their feet. Seth had barely touched his food. He felt too sick to eat. He tried to let the shushing of the waves and the squawking of the seagulls calm him down. It wasn't working.

'I still can't believe they're here,' said Seth.

'And that they've teamed up with Steele,' Angelo replied. 'That's the worst thing.'

'That is pretty bad,' added Laura.

'At least we're all here,' said Beefy. 'At least no one misses out on the tournament now.'

'But they'll hate us,' Seth pointed out. 'D'you reckon they'll want to play with us again, when we get back home?'

Beefy made a 'hmm' noise and stared at his chips, before shovelling another handful into his mouth.

'All I want to know is how they found out,' said Logan. 'Who told them?'

Seth stared at the others. He hadn't said anything to anyone. He wouldn't have dared. He stared at Angelo, Beefy, Laura and Logan, examining their faces for any giveaway signs of guilt. His eyes stopped on Alan Block, who was sucking the vinegar off his chips, in his own weird little world.

'You can tell us, Al,' said Seth. 'It doesn't matter now. It's done. We won't kick off.'

'What doesn't matter?' asked Alan. He turned to Laura. 'What's done?'

'Did you tell anyone about the tournament?'

'No way,' he told her. 'It was a top secret mission. Wasn't it, Seth?'

Seth nodded. 'No one'll be mad if you did spill,' he said.

'Why does everyone always think it's me? I never said anything to anyone. Well, not except Shlumpy...'

'Who?' asked Logan.

'Shlumpy,' repeated Alan Block.

'It's his puppet,' Seth told him.

'Okaaay,' said Logan.

'And Shlumpy wouldn't say anything, would he?' asked Alan.

'No,' said Seth. 'But you might, when you had

your hand up Shlumpy's butt!'

'It wasn't me,' Alan insisted. 'I pinky sweared.'

'He did pinky swear,' added Laura.

Alan Block stared at Seth through his tiny little eyes. He looked like he was about to bawl.

'If he says he didn't say anything, he didn't say anything,' said Angelo.

Seth nodded, sighing long and hard. Alan Block did seem like he was telling the truth. 'Who then?' he asked. 'How did they find out?'

'It could've been anyone,' Angelo replied. 'Maybe Steele heard us himself – I mean he was sneaking around the other day.'

'He was,' said Beefy.

'Was he?' asked Logan.

Seth thought about being in the playground and spotting Steele spying on them from behind that wall. He nodded.

'Maybe that was it, then,' suggested Logan.

'Maybe,' Seth replied.

'Either way it's done,' said Laura.

'Yep,' agreed Angelo. 'It is what it is.'

'Ooh look,' said Alan Block. 'A sea monster!'

He ran over to dark pile of curls and tendrils, lying there on the beach.

'It's seaweed,' Seth told him. 'Seaweed.'

'So what do we do now, though?' asked Beefy.

'What can we do?' said Seth. 'If the other

Freaks are with Steele, that makes them the enemy. Only thing we can do now is beat them.'

THE MERGER

The following day, once Seth had patched things up with his dad, Steve led his team down to the beach for a pre-tournament training session. Seth liked being at the coast, usually. They lived in the middle of the country, so it wasn't somewhere he got to go to all that often. But the dark sea and the sunny blue sky, as pretty as they were, were all wasted on him. He felt so miserable, he didn't think that any amount of beautiful scenery would cheer him up. He could've been in a Caribbean paradise and he would have still felt like poop. What had he done? Had he destroyed Freaks United before they'd even really started?

'I'll be honest with the lot of you,' said Steve. 'I'm not happy.'

'We know, Dad,' moaned Seth.

'And I'm especially not happy with you.'

'Don't be sad, Mr Hart,' said Alan Block, who

refused to call Steve 'Steve', no matter how many times he was told it was OK. 'We didn't mean to make you sad.'

'I know, Big Al. You're OK, mate,' Steve told him. 'Right, I want fifty push-ups from each of you.'

'Fifty?' moaned Logan. 'We only usually do twenty-five.'

'Well, today you're doing fifty.'

Seth and his mates clambered down onto the sand and began doing their push-ups.

'And after that, it'll be a fifty burpees,' Steve told them. 'And fifty squats...'

'All right, all right,' said Seth. 'We get it.'

'I don't quite think you do,' said Steve.

Seth thought it might be fun training on the beach. It wasn't. It was way worse than on the field. The sand made everything slower and heavier. Fifty push-ups felt like five hundred. Fifty burpees felt like a thousand. But he didn't moan about the extra warm-up exercises Steve made him do. He just did them. He deserved them. Not even the sight of Alan Block's polka dot boxer shorts, whenever he jumped up from a burpee, brightened Seth up.

When Seth and the others were having a water break, Seth noticed someone jogging over. Mr Cotton. He didn't have Steele or any of the other Freaks with him. He was on his own. Beefy looked so happy and excited, Seth thought he might pass out.

'All right?' said Mr Cotton. 'Putting these lot through their paces, I see.'

Steve nodded. 'Something like that.'

'We didn't get to meet properly,' said Mr Cotton. He held his hand out to Steve. 'I'm Leon.'

Steve shook his hand. 'I'm Steve, Seth's dad. I run Freaks United, the eleven-a-side team.' He glanced at Seth when he said 'eleven-a-side'.

'I know, I know, yeah,' said Mr Cotton. 'The others have been singing your praises, telling me what a good coach you are.'

That was something, thought Seth. He could cope with the others hating him. But the thought that his dad was in some way involved with this betrayal... that was pretty awful.

'It was all my idea,' Seth told him, just to make certain things were clear. 'Dad didn't know that we hadn't told the others about the tournament.'

'OK,' said Mr Cotton. 'I got that.'

'It's all a bit of a mess,' Steve pointed out.

'Yeah,' replied Mr Cotton. 'It is. But I think I need to take some responsibility.'

'You?' asked Steve. 'For what?'

'Well, I encouraged the lads. I saw them

talking about the tournament and I told them they should go for it.'

'But you didn't tell them to lie,' said Steve.

'No,' replied Mr Cotton. 'I didn't tell them to do that.'

'Maybe we could just combine teams?' suggested Steve. 'Get all the Freaks back together?'

Mr Cotton nodded, but before he could say anything, someone shouted out, 'COTTON, WHAT ARE YOU PLAYING AT?'

It was Mr Steele. Who else? Back in his old City shirt and his short little shorts. His big belly wobbled as he hurried across the sand. The woman with the trendy red hair was behind him, as well as the rest of the Freaks.

'Great,' said Seth. 'This is all we need.' He stared down at the twinkling sand beneath his feet. He still couldn't look at Sam and Curtis and the others.

The red-haired woman stood alongside Steele and Seth noticed his dad give her the slightest of smiles. Steve hadn't had a girlfriend for years. Seth always thought he was too busy, or maybe had a secret one. Seth did remember that his dad liked a woman on TV with red hair. Mr Steele's wife was probably his dad's type. But Seth wasn't sure if his dad had smiled because he fancied her or just felt bad for her being with Mr Steele. Probably a bit of both.

'Why did you run off?' asked Mr Steele, panting and out of breath.

'I've just been talking to Steve here,' Mr Cotton told him. 'We were wondering whether it might be a good idea to merge the two teams.'

'Merge?' asked Steele, still panting. 'Did you just say merge?'

Mr Cotton frowned at Steve. 'Yeah – merge – it means to like—'

'I know what it means,' hissed Steele. 'My lot don't want to merge, do you?'

Seth looked over at Sam and the others. No one moved or said a word.

'See,' said Steele. 'They're not interested.'

'Are you sure?' asked Mr Cotton. 'It'll be fun.'

'There are too many players,' Steele told him.

'We could rotate them in and out,' suggested Steve.

'Yeah,' said Mr Cotton. 'I like a bit of squad rotation. Good idea, Steve.'

'Good idea, Steve,' repeated Steele, mimicking Mr Cotton.

'So you don't think it's a good idea?' Mr Cotton asked.

'No, son,' Steele told him. 'I don't. The whole point was to give this lot...' He gestured behind him with his thumb to Sam and the others. 'Give them their chance to shine, to step out of the shadows. They've been betrayed. We have to begin that process of healing.'

'Betrayed's a bit strong,' said Mr Cotton. 'They're only kids.'

'Were you ever a child?' asked Steele. 'Huh, were you?'

'Well, yeah, but...'

'Were you ever betrayed?' interrupted Steele. 'Were you ever betrayed as a child?'

Mr Cotton shrugged. 'I s'pose.'

'You suppose?' asked Steele.

'Well, yeah, then,' said Mr Cotton.

'Hurt, didn't it? Still hurts, doesn't it?' And now it seemed Steele wasn't talking about Mr Cotton at all.

Mr Cotton didn't even attempt to answer. It was as though he'd seen there was no point and he'd just given up.

'There'll be no merging,' declared Mr Steele, sensing his victory. 'Now, if you'd be so kind, there's work to do.'

'Right, yeah,' replied Mr Cotton. He turned to Steve. 'I'm sorry about... well...'

'No worries.'

'Good luck,' said Mr Cotton. 'At the tournament.' He nodded at Seth and the others and trudged away with Steele and his wife and the rest of the Freaks.

'I've arranged a proper training venue,' Seth heard Steele tell Mr Cotton as he walked away. 'None of this backwater beach nonsense.'

BOYS IN THE BRANCHES

Back at the hotel, Seth and his mates sat around in his basic little room. Seth still wasn't sure how he felt about everything. He couldn't move for the guilt. But he also felt a bit of anger. OK, what he'd done was really, really rubbish. Inexcusable. But the other Freaks – Sam and the rest of them – they'd teamed up with Steele, their mortal enemy. And when Mr Cotton had suggested getting everyone back together, no one had said a word. Wasn't that just as bad?

'Have any of you been messing with my stuff?' asked Beefy, as he rummaged through his bag. 'I can't find my Freaks shirt.'

'It'll turn up,' Seth told him. 'And if it doesn't, you'll be in the donkey costume next training session!'

Beefy continued to hunt through his bag.

'I know what we did was pretty bad,' said Seth. 'But what's worse, coming here without them, or teaming up with Steele?'

'Steve even said we could get everyone back together too,' added Laura. 'So it's not like we didn't try.'

'Exactly,' Seth agreed.

'We're better off without them anyway,' said Logan. 'If they think they can beat us, they must be mad.'

'Exactly,' said Seth again, less sure how exact that was this time.

'So d'you reckon we can take them?' asked Beefy.

'All day,' replied Logan.

For the first time in quite a while Seth thought about winning the five-a-side tournament and meeting Jesse Walters. He thought about getting that trial with United and what this was all really about. 'We have to,' Seth told him.

'But you know what Steele's like,' said Angelo. 'He'll probably have some trick up his sleeve, won't he?'

'He might,' Seth replied. 'But so will we. Alan, I've got a mission for you.'

'Ooh,' said Alan Block, all excited. 'What sort of mission?'

'A spying mission,' Seth told him.

'Sweet,' said Angelo. 'I'll help.' He held his hand up for Alan to high-five him.

Alan Block swung his hand at Angelo, but completely missed, nearly hitting Angelo in the face.

'Pretty slick, you two,' said Seth sarcastically.

'Sorry,' said Alan, 'can I try again?'

Angelo held his hand up again, but this time grabbed a hold of Alan's hand and guided it onto his own. 'I'll show you how to do a high-five,' Angelo told him.

Angelo and Alan Block returned with the info pretty quickly.

'Mission possible,' said Angelo, thinking he sounded dead clever.

'Yeah?' asked Seth. 'You know where they are?'

'We do,' Angelo replied. 'It was a tricky little mission, wasn't it, Al?'

Alan just grinned.

'Quite dangerous really,' Angelo went on. 'I mean, some of the things—'

'Where are they?' Seth interrupted.

'On a field,' Alan replied matter of factly. 'Ryo – the one who likes clowns – he told us.'

'Sounds dangerous,' said Laura with a sarcastic smirk.

Now the real mission began.

The gang made their way across town to a

playing field, which was surrounded by a red running track. A row of tall oak trees stood beyond the track. Steele, Mr Cotton and the other Freaks were already out on the field. Seth knew they'd have to get to those trees to get a better view of the action.

'This was my idea,' bragged Angelo, as the six kids crept behind an old wooden hut and past the chain-link fences that surrounded a few tennis courts.

'How was it?' asked Seth. 'It was my idea.'

'The first time,' said Angelo. 'The first time we did it.'

Seth thought about the last time they'd spied on the school team. How they'd hid in the bushes and how Beefy's farts had got them all caught.

'Best behaviour, Beefs,' Seth told him.

'What?' said Beefy. 'I'm always on my best behaviour.'

Angelo pointed at the line of trees. 'We could hide up there. We'll be close enough to do some good spying. It'll be perfect.'

'*Up* there?' asked Seth.

'That's right,' said Angelo.

Seth pulled a face, unsure of the brilliance of the plan, but Angelo was already scrambling towards the trees.

'Are we actually doing this?' asked Laura.

'Like, *actually*?'

'I know,' said Logan. 'This is proper dumb. As if I'm climbing some tree, getting all bugs and stuff in my hair.'

'We've gotta do what we've gotta do,' Seth told them. 'That's what Freaks do.'

'I so knew you were spying on us that time,' said Logan.

'Big deal,' replied Seth. 'All the best teams do it – it's called scouting.'

'All the big teams hide up trees do they?' asked Laura.

Even though the sun was shining down, Seth could feel himself growing hot with embarrassment. 'Tell you what,' said Seth. 'If you're so scared, why don't you wait here and keep watch?'

'Yeah, Seth,' replied Laura. 'I'm *really* scared.'

Seth knew this was pretty lame and pretty childish. But he wanted to beat the other Freaks so badly, if this was what he had to do, he'd do it. He followed Angelo, Beefy and Alan Block towards the line of trees. When he got to the bottom of the nearest oak tree, Angelo was helping Beefy up into the branches. Angelo looked in pain, straining as he lifted Beefy's foot, pushing him up. Beefy huffed and puffed, pulling himself up into the thick branches.

Seth looked around quickly. 'Where's Alan?' he asked.

'Psst,' said someone from above.

Seth looked up and saw Alan Block up in the branches, waving at him. 'It's me, Alan.'

Seth nodded. He could see that.

'Where are Laura and Logan?' asked Angelo, once Beefy was safely up in the tree.

'They thought this was too lame,' Seth told him.

'Losers,' said Angelo.

'No, Ange, I think that's us.'

'How d'you figure?'

'Because we're hiding in a tree, spying on people,' Seth told him. 'I think that's the definition of being a loser.'

'No way,' said Angelo. 'Being a spy's well cool, am I right, Big Al?'

'You're not wrong,' answered Alan Block. And then his arm slipped and he nearly fell out of the tree. He might've if Beefy hadn't held onto him.

'I thought this was your idea anyway,' said Angelo.

'Not this,' Seth replied. 'Not climbing up trees.'

Angelo shook his head then lifted himself up into the branches of the tree. Seth looked back over at Logan and Laura, who were laughing, gesturing for him to climb. Seth growled. What was he even doing? Then he grabbed the branches and pulled himself up too.

The four of them quietened down and watched Steele's training session. It was a good position, about twenty metres from one of the goal lines. The Freaks were wearing the proper Freaks United strip – shirts with red and black stripes, back shorts, red socks. As much as Seth didn't want to admit it, they looked the business. He wished he was out there with them, instead of hiding up a stupid tree.

Out on the field, Steele was in his usual extra short shorts. But he wasn't his usual shouty self, yelling things like, 'YOU USELESS MORON!' or, 'MY NAN'S GOT A BETTER SHOT THAN THAT!' Instead, Mr Cotton was shouting words of encouragement to the players like, 'GOOD PASS, SAM!' or, 'NICE EFFORT, RYO!'

Seth was confused. He still remembered the way the school team looked when they played for Steele. Heads down, shoulders sagged, as miserable as mould. But this wasn't like that now. The other Freaks seemed like they were having fun. That was the last thing Seth wanted. If they had too much fun, they might never want to play for Freaks United again. They might even start their own team when they got home. A shiver rolled down Seth's back. He squirmed, as though the thought was some bug on his body. And then he remembered he was in a tree and squirming about probably wasn't the best idea.

'They're having way more fun than I imagined,' said Beefy.

'You're telling me,' Seth replied.

'Do you really think Steele's changed?' asked Beefy.

'It's Mr Cotton,' said Angelo. 'He's loads nicer than Steele.'

'He's the best,' Beefy added.

It was true, he was. To be honest, it would have been hard not to be nicer than Steele. But Mr Cotton was the exact opposite. Friendly, helpful, supportive, cool. As far as teachers went, Seth didn't imagine you could find a better one. And as much as he didn't want to admit it, he was jealous that Sam and the others were out there being coached by Mr Cotton. He seemed like he could get the best out of people – like a proper teacher should. What if he harnessed Curtis's speed, or used Tall John's height effectively? What if he switched Scary Alex into beast mode or got Big Sam playing like a demon in goal. Mr Cotton was the type of coach you'd want to do your best for.

Angelo pulled his phone out of his pocket and pointed it towards the field.

'What you doing?' asked Beefy.

'I'm filming,' Angelo told him. 'It's what spies do, remember.'

'We didn't even look at the stuff last time,' said Seth.

'We might this time, analyse it and that.'

'Guys,' said Beefy.

'Can we all just be quiet for a minute?' asked Seth.

'Guys...' Beefy repeated.

'What?' snapped Seth.

'I think one's coming,' Beefy told him.

'One what?' asked Seth.

'Y'know,' said Beefy. 'One.'

'Uh oh,' said Angelo. 'A big one?'

Beefy nodded, his forehead glistening with sweat.

'Just hold it,' Seth told him.

'I don't think I can,' Beefy replied.

'You better not,' said Seth. 'Not like last time.'

'Please don't,' said Angelo.

'I'm trying, I'm trying!'

'W–what happened last time?' asked a nervous Alan Block, all stuttery and scared-sounding.

'Beefy dropped a couple of bombs,' Seth told him.

'Atomic bombs,' added Angelo.

'Bombs?' asked Alan, his voice high-pitched and full of confusion.

'Farts,' whispered Seth.

'Ohhh,' said Alan. He smiled as everything made sense. Then he stopped smiling. 'Are you going to drop some bombs now?'

The four of them were so wrapped up in their conversation that they hadn't noticed Laura and Logan across the field, waving at them, trying to get their attention. And they certainly hadn't noticed the ball roll under the tree where they were hiding. Just like it had done when they first spied on the school team.

'Err, hello?' asked a voice.

Seth instantly froze and went silent. He put his finger over his lips, warning the others to be silent and still too.

'Is that you, Seth?' asked the voice.

Seth turned his eyes to the ground. Curtis was standing there, in his Freaks kit, holding a football.

Alan Block gave him a little wave and said, 'Hiya.'

Seth swatted Alan's hand down.

'Guys,' moaned Beefy, his face all screwed up. 'It's really hurting now.'

Seth knew the game was up. There was no

point trying to hide any more. 'Ahh, man, just do it.'

And Beefy just did it. He let go of the stinkiest, smelliest bomb anyone had ever smelt in the history of life. Seth thought he was going to be sick, even though they were outside in the fresh air. He held a hand over his face to shield himself from the smell.

Beefy's face had relaxed now. 'That's better.'

'Better?' said Seth, his words muffled by the hand covering his face. 'There's nothing *better* about that!'

'Smells like dead animals,' said Angelo.

'Or Sugar Puffs,' added Alan Block, and Angelo 'hmm'ed' and nodded.

Then came another voice from the bottom of the tree. 'Lads, what you doing up there?'

Seth stared down and saw Mr Cotton standing by Curtis now. Then he covered his face. 'And what's that smell? That's rank.'

'Sorry,' said Beefy.

And then Mr Steele was there too, the final piece in this awful jigsaw. 'Just ignore them,' Steele told him. 'They're spying like they always do.' He led Curtis away from the tree, back onto the field, where Sam and the others were all standing, watching.

Mr Cotton stared up at the boys. The look on

his face told Seth Mr Cotton wasn't sure at all what was going on.

'Sorry,' said Beefy. 'I think I need to go again.'

THE GHOST NEST

That afternoon, Seth and the others were back in their room at the creepy hotel getting ready for the tournament and doing their best to recover from the embarrassment of getting caught spying again. Seth opened his suitcase and started rummaging about, but he couldn't find his Freaks United shirt. It was nowhere to be seen. 'Have one of you lot nicked my shirt?' asked Seth.

'Have you nicked mine?' asked Angelo.

'I told you,' said Beefy. 'I couldn't find mine either. Maybe someone's been in our room?'

'Don't be stupid,' snapped Seth. 'Who'd do something like that?'

Beefy lifted and lowered one shoulder and made that 'I dunno' sound. 'People are weird.'

There was a knock at the door. 'Can we come in?' asked Alan Block from the other side of the door. 'You're not in your rudie nudies are you?'

'No,' said Seth. 'No rudie nudies.'

The door opened and Alan Block, Logan and Laura hurried in, looking all worried and panicked.

'We think there's a ghost,' said Alan.

'No, we don't,' said Laura.

'That's what we said.'

'No,' replied Logan. 'That's what *you* said.'

'Our Freaks shirts have gone missing,' Laura told them.

'Ours too,' said Seth.

'I think it's a ghost,' whispered Alan Block. 'Nothing else could explain it.'

'I'm sure there are lots of things that could explain it,' Seth told him.

'Name one.'

'We've all just... I dunno... misplaced them.'

'What, all of us, all at the same time?' asked Laura.

When she put it like that, it didn't seem very likely. 'But more chance than a ghost,' Seth pointed out. 'Surely?'

'Look around,' said Alan Block. 'Can't you sense it?'

'Sense what?' asked Beefy, sounding scared. He looked at Seth with his eyebrows right up on his forehead and nodded to Alan. 'What's he on about?'

THE GHOST NEST

Seth looked around the room, from the swirly carpet to the bobbly walls.

'Don't worry, Beef-stew,' Alan said. 'Ghosts won't hurt you.'

'Won't they?' asked Angelo. 'I thought that was the whole point?'

Alan Block shook his head. 'No, no,' he replied like he was some sort of expert. 'They're quite friendly really. Have you never seen *Casper*?'

Everyone just stared at one another.

'The cartoon?' asked Logan.

Alan Block just nodded, like there was nothing strange about the suggestion that *Casper* was a realistic depiction of actual ghosts.

'So, what would a ghost want with our footie shirts?' asked Seth.

'They could be having a joke on us,' Alan told him. 'Funning us. Or they... I dunno, they could be fans of Freaks United. Or making a nest. Using our shirts to make a ghost nest.'

'A ghost nest?' asked Seth.

'It's a thing.'

'I'm not sure it is.'

Suddenly, a shape appeared at the door and there was a loud knock.

Everyone jumped.

Steve stuck his head inside and peered around. 'What you lot doing?' he asked. 'We don't have long.'

'We can't find our shirts,' Seth told him.

'What, all of you?' asked Steve.

'We think a ghost's taken them,' said Alan Block. He whispered the next bit: 'For their ghost nest.'

Steve blinked a few times, like a computer trying to process information. 'Well, just grab something. All of you. We need to move.'

ONLY ONE FREAKS UNITED

They each grabbed a red T-shirt, or the closest thing they had to that and piled into the minibus. Seth already knew they'd be a laughing stock. Alan Block grabbed his red jumper with a black cat's face on the front and no body attached. It looked ridiculous. Once they were in the minibus, Steve put his foot down and sped all the way along the coast to the venue.

When they pulled up, the place was buzzing with kids of all ages, sizes and colours, most of them in football strips. There were about six or seven five-a-side 3G pitches, each divided by metal fencing. Teams were already out there, warming up, and parents and adults lined the sides of the pitches. The smell of the burger van made Seth feel hungry for the first time in ages. Now he was here, seeing all these other players and teams, Seth wondered whether his team really would have any chance of winning.

Maybe this whole thing, all the trouble he'd caused, really hadn't been worth it.

Steve led the team over to a bearded man dressed in short-sleeved shirt and wearing a red tie. 'We'd like to register our team for the tournament,' said Steve. 'D'you know where we need to go?'

The bearded man looked at his watch. 'Cutting it fine.'

'There's still time,' said Steve. 'Freaks United – that's our team name.'

'Freaks United,' repeated Beardie and he leafed through pieces of paper attached to his clipboard. 'We've already got a Freaks United.'

'That's not possible,' Steve told him.

'I think you'll find it's very possible,' Beardie replied. He turned the clipboard around to Steve and showed him just how possible it was. 'What are the odds, heh?'

Seth felt like he's been punched in the stomach.

'They've taken our name, Dad,' he said. 'Steele and the others.'

Seth watched as Steve's jaw tightened.

'You can use another name,' suggested Beardie. 'Freaks something else... Wanderers, FC, Rovers.'

'I've got one,' said Angelo. 'Ninjas FC!'

'Not this again,' moaned Seth, remembering the idiotic suggestions for team names back when it all started.

'What? It's a good name. Am I right, Alan?'

Alan Block nodded enthusiastically and the pair attempted a high-five.

'Ooh,' said Alan. 'How about the Happy Friendship Gang?'

'We're a football team!' Seth cried. 'Not a kids' TV show.'

'What're we going with then?' asked Beardie. 'Ninjas FC or Happy Friendship Gang?'

Laura rolled her eyes. 'Is that the best we can do?'

Beardie looked at his watch again in an over-exaggerated manner to let everyone know just how little time they had left.

'Just put Ninjas FC,' Seth told him.

'Get in!' Angelo did a little fist pump.

'Ninjas FC it is,' said Beardie. 'May the force be with you.'

'That's *Star Wars*,' Alan Block pointed out, sounding disgusted. 'Not ninjas.'

'You know what I meant – space ninjas.'

'No,' replied Alan. 'Not really...'

He was about to carry on the argument, but Steve put his hands on Alan's shoulders and eased him away.

'I can't believe they stole our name,' said Seth.

'It was their name too, I guess,' said Logan. Seth was surprised by his show of understanding. Maybe even Logan thought they deserved another setback?

'That was *my* name, I came up with that name.'

'It does feel like a bit of bad karma,' said Steve.

'What's that s'posed to mean?' snapped Seth.

'What goes around, comes around,' Steve told him. 'That's what they say.'

Seth grimaced. First Logan, now his dad. 'I know I messed up, d'you have to keep going on?'

Just at that moment, Mr Steele appeared, all smiles and laughter. And small shorts. 'How do,' he said, giving them all the cheesiest of grins. 'So, what name did you decide on?'

No one said anything.

'If you'd have got here a bit earlier... oh well, never mind. Early bird catches the worm and all that.'

Seth had had enough. There was no way Mr Steele had turned over a new leaf. He was the worm – the biggest, baldest, slyest worm going. Worms didn't turn over new leaves. They didn't have any arms. So they couldn't even if they wanted to. This was all about revenge.

'So, is everyone ready for the tournament?'

Steele asked them.

Again no one answered. And now Beardie had appeared at Steele's side. 'You're with the other Freaks, aren't you?' he asked.

'*Freaks United*,' said Steele, emphasising the words to really it rub in. 'That's right, yes.'

'This team were after the same name,' Beardie told him. 'Who'da thunk it. Two Freaks Uniteds in the same tournament!'

'We're actually the same Freaks United,' Steele told the man, with a smirk. 'Or at least we were.'

'Oh right,' replied Beardie. 'So there's a bit of rivalry here, then, is there?'

'Something like that,' said Steve.

Seth saw that his dad was giving the PE teacher a proper death stare. He wondered if a karate chop was on Steve's mind right now.

'Well, a bit of good-natured ribbing never hurt anyone.' Beardie nodded at Steele and Steve and wandered off, his clipboard clasped behind his back.

Steele just stood there, grinning at Steve.

'I think it's time you moved on as well,' said Steve.

Seth eyed them both. He imagined his dad launching himself at Steele, shouting 'Hiii-yahh!' Right now, Seth really wanted him to do it too.

'Right you are,' replied Steele. 'Come along, Julie.'

Steele's red-haired wife smiled at them all. She was wearing almost as colourful clothes today. A bright green vest top, white jeans, golden sandals. Laura was right. What was someone like her doing with Mr Steele? She looked happy and nice. The complete opposite of Steele. Seth saw her smile at Steve before she followed Steele off into the crowd of parents and kids.

Seth wasn't sure which he hated more. The old, sadistic Steele or this new and 'improved' fake nicey-nice version exacting his revenge. Actually, definitely the new improved one. Steele's grand revenge plan was going like a dream. They'd even lost the team name. Seth had a sinking feeling. He wondered if there was anything Ninjas FC could do about it.

THE OTHER FREAKS

'John's in goal,' said Steve. 'Interesting.'

John always played up front for Freaks. He was so tall he always got the flick-ons and knock downs. But there wasn't much use for that stuff with five-a-side. The ball wasn't supposed to go above head height. Seth and his teammates stood at the sidelines and watched as the other Freaks played their first match. Tall John was in goal. Alex and Sam were playing in defence. Brooke was in midfield, with Curtis up front.

'I still can't believe Brooke came along too,' said Laura. 'I've messaged her loads and she just keeps ignoring me. We're s'posed to be best mates. She's only playing for the team because I got her into it.'

Seth felt exactly the same. They were all only there because he brought them together. Him, Beefy and Angelo. They were the ones who'd scouted them and jumped through all sorts of crazy hoops to convince them to play for Freaks, then turned them into half-decent players. And now it was like they didn't even know each other. They were all out there, laughing and joking, having the time of their lives, enjoying their football, just like they did when Freaks played the school team. Just like they did at every training session. Seth felt hot with anger.

Then Alex played a ball across the pitch. Curtis took it on his in-step, giving himself a little bit of space. Then he hit, hard and low. It arrowed right into the top corner. He hit it so hard, the ball got stuck in the corner of the goal frame.

Steve clapped and called out, 'Good goal, Curt!' while the other Freaks celebrated around him. It wasn't right, watching them score and play and have fun without him. Seth felt like he was being left out. And he understood exactly how the other Freaks must've all felt when they found he was taking half the team to a tournament and they weren't invited. It felt rubbish. Totally and utterly rubbish.

When the ref blew the final whistle after thirty minutes, the other Freaks had won 5–1. As much as it hurt Seth to admit it, they were good. *Really* good. They played the sort of football he wanted to play and they did it with a smile on their faces. If Seth and Ninjas FC were going to have any chance of winning this tournament and meeting Jesse Walters, they were going to have to be better than the other Freaks. And as things stood, that didn't look easy. Seth wondered if he even cared about meeting Jesse Walters now, anyway.

Steele led his team off the pitch and over to Julie, who was with Mr Cotton, handing them all water bottles. 'Well done *team*,' said Steele, emphasising the word 'team' and staring at Seth as he said it.

Suddenly, Seth had an idea. If he could show the other Freaks what Steele was up to, they might quit Steele's team. Then again, maybe they wouldn't. Maybe they were all in on it too, and all they wanted to do was show Seth and the 'chosen ones' they were just as good themselves, if not better. Seth knew exactly how that felt. It was the same feeling that inspired him to start Freaks United in the first place.

'Good work,' Mr Cotton told the other Freaks, but there was nothing snide in his words, as there had been in Steele's. Mr Cotton sounded genuine, filled with warmth and encouragement.

'Well played, Alex,' said Julie. 'You were really good.'

Alex grinned at Mr Steele's wife as he sucked

on a water bottle.

Then Mr Steele came over to Seth and Steve and the others. Seth could tell by the look on his face, he was loving this. Milking it for everything he could.

Steve stood there, with his hands on his hips.

'Not a bad performance, that,' Mr Steele said. 'You've trained them well.' He winked at Steve. 'So when you lot up?'

Steve checked his watch. 'We're on in five minutes.'

'Is that what you're playing in?' asked Steele. 'No proper shirts?'

Steve ignored him.

'Right, come on,' said Steve. 'Best get you lot ready.'

Steve led Seth and the others over to another playing surface, three pitches away. Seth looked back at the other Freaks as they laughed and congratulated one another. All back-patting and high-fives. Just like the school team had when they'd been picked and Seth and his mates hadn't.

'Look at them,' said Angelo.

Seth saw Sam whisper something to Brooke and the pair of them laughed.

'Just because they won a game,' Angelo went on. 'Big deal.'

'Yeah, did you see them?' asked Beefy. 'Laughing and joking, trying to wind us up?'

'I bet it was them who nicked our shirts,' said Seth.

'How would they have?' asked Beefy.

'Who knows, but they're in the same hotel. And did you see the way Steele looked when he was going on about it? All smug.' The more Seth thought about it, the more wound up he felt. The other Freaks had stolen their name. They'd probably stolen their shirts too. And now they were having a good laugh at Seth's expense.

'It's not right,' said Beefy. 'This was s'posed to be fun.'

'Doesn't feel like it,' said Logan, sulkily. 'I thought we were gonna win this thing.'

'We will,' Seth told him, even though he didn't believe his own words. 'And as soon as we do, we'll rub that lot's noses in it!'

Out of nowhere, Alan Block cheered. 'Wahey!' He stretched his hand out, palm down. 'Let's all put our hands in.'

The others just started at him.

'I don't think we will actually,' said Seth.

It felt like they were at rock bottom.

FREAKS DIVIDED

Ninjas FC sucked big time. There were no smiles on any of their faces. They weren't having fun. And it showed in their football. Their tackles were tame. Their passing was poor. Their shooting was shoddy. It was lucky they *were* actually decent players, because they were still winning. Just about. They won their first game thanks to some heroics in goal from Beefy, a long-ranger from Laura and a big fat chunk of luck. In their second game, they'd only just managed another one–nil win when Seth scored with pretty much the last kick. They were really struggling.

Their third mini-league game wasn't any different. In fact, they were playing even worse than before. Their tackles were terrible. Their passing was pathetic. And as for their shooting, well, that was beyond shoddy. It was a shambles.

All the while, Seth was trudging around the

pitch snarling and growling like an angry pitbull. He was shouting at his teammates, demanding the ball, calling them names when he didn't get it. He called Beefy a 'useless waste of space', he called Angelo 'a liability' and he called Logan a 'pathetic poseur'. He knew he was being an idiot, but he couldn't help it. He wanted to win so badly. And it wasn't just about Jesse Walters and a United trial any more. Now he wanted to show the other Freaks they should've stayed at home. He wanted to beat them. At any cost.

They were lucky to get to half-time with the score still at nil–nil. Without Beefy, they'd have been three or four down.

Steve took Ninjas FC to one side for a team talk. 'What's the matter with you all?' he asked. 'You're top of your league. You should be enjoying yourselves. And you've all got faces on you like a wet weekend.'

No one really said anything, they just sucked water from their bottles.

'Come on,' said Steve. 'What's got into you all?'

'It's these lot,' Seth told him.

'Us lot?' asked Angelo.

'You're not passing to me.'

'Yeah, because you're being a complete idiot,' said Laura.

'How am I?' snapped Seth.

'The way you're going on,' Laura snapped back. 'Shouting at everyone all the time, like you're so much better than the rest of us.'

'I'm just trying to get you all going,' Seth told her.

'You're shutting us down,' said Logan.

'I want to win, what's wrong with that?'

'You don't seem very happy, Seth,' said Alan Block quietly. 'You seem a bit of an angry-pants.'

'He's right,' Steve agreed. 'Maybe not the pants bit, but you're definitely not yourself.'

'How did I know you'd defend everyone else instead of me?' asked Seth.

'That's not fair,' said Steve. 'Not fair at all.'

'I'll tell you what's not fair. Me having to play with this lot.'

'That's enough,' Steve told him. 'Think about what you're saying.'

Seth saw the sad looks on Angelo and Beefy's faces, the scowls on Logan and Laura's. He knew he'd gone too far. But it didn't feel like there was any way back. So he kept on going: 'I just want to win,' said Seth. 'I'm sick of being a loser all the time.'

'You've just won three in a row,' said Steve.

'Barely,' muttered Seth.

'So we're all losers?' asked Angelo.

Seth stared at his mate. Stared at them all. 'Yeah. Yeah you are.'

'That's enough,' said Steve.

'Yeah, man,' said Logan. 'Listen to your dad.'

'Keep your nose out,' Seth told him. 'I'm not talking to you.'

'Who d'you think you are?' asked Logan. 'Going on the way you are?'

'Who d'you think *you* are?' asked Seth. 'You're not even a *real* Freak.'

'You what?' demanded Logan.

'You heard,' hissed Seth. 'I didn't even...'

'You didn't even what?'

'Doesn't matter,' Seth told him, staring Logan in the eyes.

'Lads, lads...' said Steve, doing his best to intervene.

'No, go on,' said Logan.

'I didn't even want you to join,' Seth told him. 'It was them...' He gestured to Angelo and Beefy with a flick of his head. 'Not me.'

'We need to quit this right now,' said Steve.

'Well we don't want you,' said Logan, with an extreme pout.

'As if.'

'Ask them. Ask them if you don't believe me.'

Seth looked around at his teammates. 'That right?' asked Seth. 'You want me out?'

Beefy smiled sadly. Angelo turned away. Alan Block smiled awkwardly like he was unsure what was going on.

'So that's it?' asked Seth. 'I'm out?'

'No one said that,' said Steve.

'No one said anything!' snapped Seth desperately. He could see that he wasn't wanted. And he couldn't be there any more. So he walked away.

He heard his dad calling after him as he went. 'SETH!'

But he didn't look back.

WORDS OF WISDOM

Seth trudged along the sand alone, while Beefy and Angelo and the others went to the nearby funfair. He wouldn't have gone along with them, even if they'd have asked. As the sun set over the sea, the sky was filled with fire: oranges and reds and yellows. Seth wondered whether that was what his insides looked like – full of anger and rage. He knew why he felt so angry now; he'd been thinking about it as he stared at the sea. At first he thought it was because of the other Freaks and how much he wanted to beat them. But the more he thought about it, he realised that maybe his dream, everything he wanted – playing professional football, playing for United – maybe it was just that. A dream. He'd watched the other Freaks. He watched some of the other teams that had been playing. There were good players. Loads of them. Did Seth really have what it took to stand out? Was he really that special? Maybe he just had to accept that he wasn't that good. He was fine, he was OK. But to make it the way Jesse Walters had made it, fine and OK weren't ever going to be good enough.

Seth pulled his phone out and stared at the team photo his dad had taken back before Freaks played the school team, when they were all wearing their new football shirts. He still remembered how good that day had felt. How much he'd loved the team badge Alan had designed – the little freaky face, with one big eye and a tongue hanging out. It was still one of the most awesome things Seth had ever seen. The big grins on their faces made him smile and feel sad. They'd all been so happy. A proper team. And now look at them. They couldn't be any less of a team if they tried. And it was all down to one person and one person alone. Seth grabbed a rock from the sand and hurled it into the dark, grey sea.

'Not cold?' asked a voice.

Seth turned to find Mr Cotton standing nearby, hands in the pockets of his padded jacket and the collar zipped up around his neck.

'Huh?' said Seth.

'Aren't you cold?' repeated Mr Cotton. 'I'm freezing.'

'Yeah,' replied Seth, realising it had got pretty chilly now the sun was going down. His head had been somewhere else entirely. He hadn't even felt the cold until now.

'It's all gone a bit west?' said Mr Cotton.

Seth nodded. 'Just a bit.'

'You wanna talk about it?'

'Not really.'

'I used to be like that,' said Mr Cotton. 'When I was your age. Bottling everything up – I didn't wanna talk to anyone. Not any more though, you can't shut me up these days.' He smiled.

Seth grunted. He didn't really have anything else to say.

'What's all this really about?' asked Mr Cotton.

Seth turned to him. 'What?'

'I mean yeah, I encouraged you to come along,' said Mr Cotton. 'For the experience and that. But this seems important to you. Like really important.'

Seth looked at the young PE teacher. The whole Jesse Walters thing seemed pretty pathetic now. 'I dunno... guess I just wanted to win for once.'

'Didn't think that mattered to you lot,' said Mr Cotton. 'That's what Sam and the others said. That's why they all love being Freaks. Reckon

I'd have loved it too when I was a kid.'

'But you have to be a winner, if you want to play for United.'

'Is that what you want?' asked Mr Cotton. 'To play for United?'

'Who doesn't?'

'But I mean, is that what you *really* want?'

'Yeah,' Seth replied. But the word didn't come out right. It sounded all scratchy and wrong, so he tried again: 'Yeah.' He realised this was the first time he'd said it out loud to anyone. Now he wished he could suck it back inside him. He felt ridiculous. As if *he* could play for United.

'It's hard, playing at that level,' Mr Cotton told him. 'It's hard playing professionally at any level.'

'So I should just forget about it?' asked Seth.

'No, not at all. I'm just telling you the truth – it *is* hard.'

Seth shrugged. 'If it wasn't, everyone would do it.'

'True,' said Mr Cotton. 'Very true.'

'D'you think I'm an idiot?' asked Seth. 'Wanting that?'

'Why would I think that?'

'Because it's ridiculous, isn't it? Me playing for United? Playing for anyone, even.'

'Someone has to,' said Mr Cotton. 'People do

make it. And if it's what you want – what you *really* want – why not go for it?'

'And what if I don't make it?' asked Seth.

'Then you don't make it. But you'll never know, will you? If you don't give it a shot.'

'That's why I wanted to come here and win,' Seth told him. 'I know it sounds dumb, but I figured if we could win and get to meet Jesse Walters, he might see me play. He might've thought I was good enough, get me a trial or something.'

'OK,' said Mr Cotton, nodding. 'Makes sense. Kind of. Can I tell you something, Seth?'

'Hmm-mm.'

'I was signed to United... when I was your age, actually.'

'*United* United?' asked Seth. '*The* United.'

'Yeah,' said Mr Cotton.

'Woah.'

'I went through all the age groups, worked my backside off,' Mr Cotton told him. 'I did everything that was asked of me. Everything.'

'What happened?'

'They cut me loose,' said Mr Cotton. 'Told me I wasn't good enough. I was eighteen at the time. I was devastated, y'know – like fully gutted. I couldn't get out of bed for days. I tried out for a few other teams, but my confidence was shot.

That was that.'

'That sucks.'

'Yeah, it does,' said Mr Cotton. 'But that's the way of it. Professional football. It's a cut-throat business.'

'And now you're a teacher,' said Seth.

'I am. And d'you know what? I absolutely love it.'

'Really?' asked Seth. He couldn't imagine anything worse.

'Yeah, man. I get to work with kids like yourself, and Angelo and Sam, really good kids. And I get to make a difference, y'know. An actual difference. At the end of the day, that's all we wanna do, man. All of us. We just wanna make a difference.'

'So you're saying I should forget about being a footballer and be a teacher?' asked Seth.

Mr Cotton laughed. 'You're funny, man, y'see. What I'm saying is, if you really want something, you should go for it. But not at the expense of everything else, d'you get me? Having fun, having a life – your friends. That stuff's really important too. I mean, who you gonna celebrate all that success with if you've got no mates?'

Seth nodded, finally understanding what Mr Cotton was *really* telling him.

ON THE SIDELINES

Shortly after, Seth headed back to the Creepy Towers Hotel and got into bed. There was no one else around. Angelo and Beefy must have still been out at the funfair with the others. Seth felt awful. Everything he'd done, the way he acted was a disgrace. It wasn't on. None of it. He made up his mind; he was going to say sorry. But when Angelo and Beefy crept into the bedroom later that night, Seth just closed his eyes and rolled over, pretending to be asleep.

'Keep quiet,' whispered Angelo. 'I think he's asleep.'

'Probably best not to wake him,' said Beefy. 'He might kick off again.'

As much as he wanted to, Seth just couldn't bring himself to say sorry. It felt like things had gone too far. So he just lay there, as still as a statue.

The next day, Seth sat at the back of the minibus. All of them were still in their mismatched red shirts. Alan was still wearing his red jumper with the cat's face on it. Seth kept his head down and his thoughts to himself. He just sat there and listened as they all chatted away about nothing. He knew his outburst was still on all their minds though. He could sense it. He still hadn't said sorry. He'd already divided the Freaks in two. And now he'd become one. Even Alan Block didn't seem bothered that Seth was down in the dumps. He was too busy going on about 'ghost nests'. Mr Cotton was right. What was the point in anything if you didn't have your mates to share it with? He'd been an enormous idiot. A monumental moron. A Great. Big. Goon.

Steve led the team across the car park. There was a buzz in the air. It reminded Seth of the time his dad had taken him to Wembley to watch United in the FA cup final. Seth remembered feeling it all – the tension, nerves, excitement, expectation – all of it swirling around him inside and out. He remembered being able to tell that everyone was feeling the same, which seemed to magnify everything by ten. Of course, it wasn't *exactly* like that now. This was only a five-a-side tournament at a coastal town after all. But it was the same sort of swirly feeling.

Seth kept himself at the back of the group as Steve led Ninjas FC to the 3G pitches. In the morning there were going to be four quarter-finals, then two semi-finals after lunch, and the final in the evening.

Steve got them all together at the sideline.

'Right,' he said. 'I know it's not the same as your own kits, but I got you all these.' He pulled out a carrier bag and handed everyone a red and blue striped T-shirt. Seth unfolded his. They each had a ninja face printed on the front, outlined in white. But it wasn't just any ninja face. It was the green Freaky monster face from the badge on their Freaks shirts. Underneath the face were the words 'Ninjas FC'.

Angelo grinned from ear to ear. 'Nice one, Big Stevo,' he said. 'These are well cool.'

'Barcelona colours,' said Beefy.

'Thought you could all channel your inner Messi,' Steve winked. 'Nothing to do with the fact they were on offer. You can thank Big Al once again for the design.'

Seth watched as the others congratulated Alan Block and patted him on the back.

The T-shirts each had their nicknames on the back. Just as their Freaks United shirts had. Beefy's still said 'Beefy'. Angelo's still said 'Raging Bull'. Laura's said 'The Guv'nor'.

Logan's said 'The Man'. Alan Block's still said 'Big Al'. And Seth's still said 'Captain Hart'.

Captain Hart, thought Seth. He still thought it had that superhero ring to it. The only problem was that now, he didn't feel much like a superhero. On the super scale, he felt somewhere near the bottom – unexceptional, most probably. Or better still, really, really rubbish.

Seth watched as the others pulled the new shirts over their red ones. They all looked good. They weren't their Freaks United shirts, but they were a massive step-up from the random red T-shirts they'd worn the previous day.

Seth took a moment to talk to his dad, while the others were showing their new shirts off to one another.

'I don't deserve the nickname,' said Seth, keeping his voice low so they couldn't hear him.

'You're the heart and soul of this team,' Steve told him. 'Course you do.'

'Not any more.'

'Come on,' said Steve. 'I know what happened yesterday—'

'I was out of order.'

'You were, but we all make mistakes.'

'Feels like all I've been doing lately,' Seth muttered.

'And we have to learn to deal with the fallout, too. You're on the bench, mate.'

Seth was gutted, but he knew it was probably only fair.

'Take a picture then, Big Stevo!' said Angelo.

The team gathered in a line, arms around one another. Seth stood behind his dad, arms folded.

'You getting in or what?' Steve asked Seth.

Seth didn't want to make another scene, not after what happened yesterday, so he joined the others. But he didn't put his arm around anyone. He just stood there with his arms folded at the end, like he wasn't really part of the team at all.

Steve pulled his phone out and took aim. 'You know what to say,' he told them.

Everyone shouted, 'FREAKS!' together. Apart from Seth; he just mumbled the word like he did when he was supposed to be 'singing' in school assemblies.

Steve's phone made a clicking sound.

'We can put that on my website!' said Alan Block. 'With all the other ones. Our fans will love it!'

Seth watched the semi-final from the sidelines, stood alongside his dad. A mixture of feelings whirled inside him like a tornado. He felt annoyed at his dad for leaving him out. Angry at himself for everything he'd done. He also felt nervous. As much as he wanted to believe what Mr Cotton had said about mates coming first, he still wanted to win.

The other Freaks had already made it through to the semi-final by winning four-nil. They were on fire. They'd only conceded one goal in the whole tournament. With Steele and Cotton behind them, they were the team to beat.

The ref blew his whistle and Ninjas FC's quarter-final kicked off. Straight away Angelo, Beefy and the others looked much better. Nothing like yesterday's shambles. Seth thought they seemed much happier too – probably because he wasn't stomping about, shouting orders at everyone and calling them all 'losers'.

Laura picked up the ball at the back. She feinted left and went right, dribbling across the pitch. She made herself a yard of space and hit one. Right through the goalie's legs.

'MEGS!' shouted Angelo.

The team gathered around Laura, patted her back and high-fived her. Steve cheered and Seth even clapped his hands, pleased for his friends. Out of all the feelings mixed up inside him, right now he mostly just felt sad that he wasn't out there with them.

But things still weren't going all the Ninja's

way. Seth expected them to relax and open up, score a few more. Instead they seemed to shrink inside themselves. The other team peppered Beefy's goal with shots and if it wasn't for some brilliant keeping from the big man, quite a few last ditch tackles and a fat wedge of fortune, the opposition would've put the Ninjas out for good. Seth so wished he was out there with them, giving everything he had for the team.

When the ref finally blew his whistle, Seth could see the relief on his teammates' faces. Another one–nil victory.

'Good win,' said Steve.

'Only just,' replied Laura.

'But you stuck in,' Steve told her. 'And you deserved the result in the end. Well done.'

'Yeah, well done,' said Seth. It was the first time he'd said anything to any of them since the day before, and the words were all quiet and faint, and didn't sound like they belonged to him at all.

Angelo and Beefy nodded at him, but Seth just looked away, feeling hot and awkward.

'You all ready for a semi-final then?' asked Steve.

PENALTIES

The quarter-final was tense, but the semi-final was *really* squeaky bum time. Alford Allstars were a good side. Seth had caught their previous game while Angelo and the others had been resting. They were tough, skilled, a proper team. But it seemed like both teams were more interested in not losing than winning. Everyone was too careful, too scared to make a mistake. There was a place in the final at stake and both teams obviously wanted to be there. The other Freaks had already booked their place. Of course they had. They'd been the standout team in the tournament, smashing teams by three, four and five. Seth didn't really want to admit it, but he was worried. The other Freaks looked formidable. He also felt responsible, like he'd created this team of underdogs who were desperate to prove themselves. He'd created this monster. He felt like Dr. Frankenstein.

PENALTIES

When the ref blew for the final whistle, neither Ninjas FC nor Alford had scored. It was down to penalties.

Their striker was the first to step up.

'COME ON, BEEFS!' cheered Angelo.

Seth wanted to cheer for his mate too, but he still didn't feel a part of things. So he just bit his tongue.

Their striker took the kick.

Beefy dived. The wrong way.

1–0 to Alford.

Seth groaned.

First up for the Ninjas was Laura. She looked calm and composed, just like always. Seth was confident she'd bury her penalty. And she did. No problem.

1–1!

Laura jogged back to the halfway line, where she was congratulated by the others.

Their midfielder stepped up. Placed it right in the bottom corner. Beefy had no chance.

2–1 to Alford.

Next up for Ninjas – Logan. Seth was sure he wouldn't miss. Although a part of him – a small part – wanted him to.

He didn't.

2–2.

Logan celebrated with a little fist-pump.

Nothing over the top from him. He smoothed his hair down, making himself perfect again.

One of their defenders was up next. He was big and tall and solid. He didn't have the best technique, but that didn't stop him from burying the ball in the top right.

3–2 to Alford.

Angelo was up next for Ninjas.

'COME ON, ANGE!' shouted Steve.

'Come on, Ange,' Seth repeated, whispering to himself. Seth could tell Angelo was nervous. He was looking everywhere except the goal. Seth really wanted his mate to score. Come on, Ange. Come on, Ange. He repeated the words over and over in his head.

Angelo didn't let him down either.

3–3!

Seth bit at his thumbnail, tearing it off. This was proper tense.

The tension didn't affect the next Alford player up, though. He slammed it straight in the net.

4–3 to Alford.

And next up was Beefy. They'd had to go for him – the keeper – over Alan Block. As much as everyone loved Alan, he wasn't the first name you'd have on your list for a penalty shoot-out.

Beefy didn't mess about. He buried it.

4–4.

'Get in!' said Seth, and the others congratulated Beefy on the halfway line.

Last up for Alford was their keeper. He looked nervous, shaky. Even more nervous than Angelo had. He nodded, like he was psyching himself up. Like he was telling himself he could do this. Seth hoped that he wouldn't. If this went in, that was it. There was no way Alan Block would score. The only hope was that this guy missed, the shoot-out went to sudden-death and everyone got to go again. Seth crossed his fingers.

Their keeper hit it, low and hard.

Beefy dived. The right way this time. And he got a good hand to it, tipping it around the post.

Seth cheered and Beefy ran over to his teammates, pumping his fist. They all ruffled his hair and patted his back.

'PLAYED, BEEF!' shouted Steve.

Seth was momentarily buzzing. Until he remembered who was up next.

Alan Block looked around at Laura and the others. Even from where Seth was, he could see he looked absolutely petrified.

A couple of adults near to Seth nodded at Alan and seemed to laugh to themselves. Seth immediately felt angry. He also started to hope and believe. 'Come on, Big Al,' he whispered. 'You can do this.'

Angelo and Beefy must've been telling him the same thing, because they had their arm around him, probably trying to give him confidence.

Alan Block grabbed the ball and trudged to the edge of the box. He looked over at Steve and Seth.

'NOTHING TO WORRY ABOUT!' shouted Steve, and Seth smiled at Alan, letting him know he could do this.

An image of The Blockster swinging his foot and his shorts falling down, revealing his polka dot pants to the world, flashed through Seth's head. But he shook those negative thoughts away and repeated his mantra: 'Come on, Big Al,' he whispered. 'You can do this.'

And do you know what?

It wasn't the best of shots, but it went in!

And when it did, Seth couldn't stop himself. He lost it, running over to his teammates and hugging the life out of Alan Block. For a moment, he forgot everything. All the drama, all the aggro. He just wanted to celebrate with the others. Then he realised what he was doing, and realised everyone was staring at him.

'I'm sorry,' he told them. Ten percent of his apology was for being there when he wasn't welcome. The other ninety was for everything else.

'It's OK,' said Alan Block. 'I like being hugged. Hug me again, if you like.'

'Nah, you're OK.'

'Hug him,' said Laura. 'Go on.'

'Yeah, Seth,' added Angelo. 'Just hug him.'

And they all started chanting – Laura, Logan, Seth and Beefy: 'HUG HIM, HUG HIM, HUG HIM...'

Seth shrugged, and did his best to pretend he wasn't happy. 'Whatever'. Then he hugged Alan Block all over again. Alan hugged him back too. And so did the rest of them. Angelo, Beefy, even Laura. But not Logan. He just stood there, arms folded, shaking his head.

'I love group hugs,' said Alan. 'They're the best.'

When they all finally let go of one another, and Alan had got over the fact there wouldn't be any more hugging, Steve congratulated them. 'Nerves of steel, this lad,' said Steve, putting his arm around Alan. 'Nerves of steel.'

'Have I, Mr Hart?' asked Alan. 'Have I got nerves of steel?'

'You certainly have, Big Al,' Steve told him. 'And will you stop calling me Mr Hart?'

Alan Block just smiled.

'So,' said Steve, 'are we all friends again? Can we all move on from what happened yesterday?'

'No,' Seth told him.

The others looked at him, their faces all frowny. If anyone should have been saying they couldn't move on, it was them.

'Seth,' said Steve, unsure his son was taking the right course of action.

'Not before I've apologised properly,' Seth replied. 'I've been well out of order. Yesterday, I dunno, I just wanted to win so bad... I wasn't myself.'

'You might've been possessed by a demon,' suggested Alan Block. 'From the hotel.'

'Yeah, maybe.'

'Do you really think?' asked Alan.

'No,' said Seth matter-of-factly.

And the others laughed.

'I still can't believe we'll be playing the other Freaks,' said Beefy.

Steve had taken Seth and the team to the nearby cafe for a drink and some snacks before The Big Game.

'Wasn't gonna be any other way, was it?' said Steve.

'How d'you mean?' asked Seth.

'It's just the way these things go. It was meant

to be.'

'Like destiny?' asked Angelo.

'Exactly,' Steve nodded. 'Destiny.'

'So what's the plan then, Big Stevo?'

'I think we just keep on as we have been,' Steve told him. 'We're tight at the back, we just need to take our chances.

'Alan, you OK to be subbed off this half?' asked Steve.

'Sure thing,' said Alan Block.

'Good man,' Steve told him. 'Seth, d'you think you're ready to come back into the team?'

Angelo, Beefy and Laura turned to Seth expectantly.

Seth looked up from his chips, to see who they were talking about. When he saw they were all staring at him, he scratched his neck. 'Huh?'

'You ready to play?' asked Steve.

'In the final?' replied Seth.

'No,' said Steve. 'Over there in the corner. Of course in the final!'

'Duh brain,' said Angelo.

'Derp derp,' added Alan Block.

'All right, Big Al,' replied Seth. 'Don't get cocky.'

It was too late for that, Alan was already being cocky. So much so, he just repeated the words or the sound, or whatever it was, all over again, but really loud: 'DERP DERP!'

The other kids and adults in the cafe looked over.

'I sometimes wonder about you, bro,' said Laura.

'What?' asked Alan Block. 'I was just doing the "derp derp".'

'Seth,' said Steve, interrupting all the derping. 'Never mind all the derp derp nonsense...' Angelo and Alan snickered. 'You OK to play in the final?'

Seth inhaled a big breath, doing his best to fill his lungs with confidence. 'Yeah,' he said. 'If that's OK with everyone else?'

'Fine by me,' said Laura.

'Me too,' agreed Angelo.

'Me three,' added Beefy.

'Me four,' said Alan Block, and then fist-pumped like he'd just made the best joke ever. He was clearly happy to step aside after his heroics. Seth smiled at him.

'Dan?' asked Steve. 'OK with you?'

Logan shrugged, playing with his phone. 'Whatever, man.'

'Now, can we all put our hands in, like we do sometimes?' asked Alan. 'I know mostly everyone just says, "No, Alan, stop that with your hands", but I think we should do it this time because—'

PENALTIES

'All right, all right. Yes, jeez,' said Seth, interrupting. He put his hand on top of Alan's.

Laura put her had in too. Then Angelo and Beefy. Everyone looked expectantly at Logan. He sighed, shook his head, then reluctantly put his hand in too. 'You lot are fully lame,' he moaned.

'And you, Steve,' said Alan Block.

Steve blinked a few times, pretending to be shocked or something. 'Did he... did he just call me Steve?'

'I think he did, Big Stevo,' Angelo told him.

Steve pretended to faint, then he laughed and put his hand in too.

'On the count of three,' said Alan. 'One... Two... Three.'

Everyone shouted, 'FREAKS!' together. Everyone except Logan, who shouted, 'LAAAME-O!' But even he was laughing along.

SEEING RED

Seth led Ninjas FC out onto the pitch for the final. It was great to be back in with his mates – the best – but this was the *final*. The first final he'd ever played in in his life. His heart was banging – *BADUMP BADUMP BADUMP*. He was sweating from everywhere. His armpits. His back. His hands. He was sweating so much, even his sweat was sweating! He was a heart-thumping, sweaty, dry-mouthed mess.

Then he saw them. All standing there. Mr Steele, Mr Cotton. The other Freaks. Steele looked so smug. The other Freaks didn't look like their hearts were hammering away, or their sweat was sweating. They all seemed comfortable and relaxed, laughing and joking with one another – all there in their proper Freaks United shirts. Seth started to feel something else other than nerves. He started to feel hot and angry. Jealous. He thought the feeling had gone away, but now he was here, standing opposite them all, it was back.

He wanted to win.

Before the match, the ref made them all shake hands with one another. Sam, Curtis, Ryo, Alex – they all seemed to smile at Seth when they shook his hand. Seth snarled at them. He knew they were being smug, mocking him. Alan Block had a sense of the supernatural. Seth had a sense when he was being made a mug of.

As soon as the whistle went, Seth was running all over the pitch, flying into tackles, chasing after everything. But the other Freaks were composed and calm. The string of flawless victories had given them a lot of confidence. Every time Seth got anywhere near the ball, they knocked it around him. He couldn't get a look in.

As the half went on, Seth became more and more frustrated. He didn't give up though, he couldn't. But he started to feel like he was chasing lost causes.

Brooke volleyed a great shot and Beefy just about got his fingers to it, scooping it away. It was a brilliant save – world class probably – but Seth knew it wouldn't be long before the other Freaks went in front.

And then it happened. Tall John collected the

ball in goal and rolled it out to Alex.

Alex knocked it to Ryo, who played it through to Brooke. She pulled off a quick step-over and took the ball past Laura, who growled out in anger.

It seemed like Brooke was going to shoot, but she didn't. She pulled the ball back for Sam.

Seth grabbed onto Sam's shirt, but it didn't stop him. Sam had too much momentum. He thundered the ball at the goal.

Beefy couldn't stop the shot. Not this time. The ball flew into the top corner and smacked the metal frame at the back of the goal.

The other Freaks congratulated Sam with fist-bumps and back pats. They weren't even celebrating that much. If it had been Seth and his Ninjas, they'd have been jumping about all over the place. But it was like the other Freaks weren't all that bothered, like they expected to go out and win comfortably.

Seth could feel himself getting hotter and hotter.

When Sam jogged by and whispered, 'Unlucky, *mate*,' to Seth, that was it. The tiny little cord that was keeping his anger in check snapped. His fuses and gaskets blew. The red mist descended. He was about to go ballistic, postal, off at the deep end.

He lost it.

And now Seth wasn't thinking about scoring or winning. All he could think about was hurting Sam. Wiping that smirk off his big fat smirky face.

Just before half-time, Sam picked up the ball.

This was it. Seth's chance for revenge. And he took it.

He steamed in. Just as Sam was about to play the ball out, Seth went in hard on his shin, just the way Logan had on Seth when he'd first tried out for the school team.

Sam screamed out in pain.

Steele screamed out too. 'REFEREE! THAT'S A RED!'

The ref blew his whistle. *FWEEEE*!

Sam was on the ground clutching his shin as his teammates ran over. Brooke shoved Seth and Seth was about to shove her back, but Angelo grabbed Seth and held him.

'It's usually me who loses it,' said Angelo.

Seth shrugged his mate away and the ref called Seth over.

'I'll have none of that on my pitch, son,' the ref told him. 'What's your name?'

'Seth,' replied Seth reluctantly. 'Hart.'

The ref wrote the name down in his notepad, and put his hand into his pocket. Seth's heart descended to his trainers. He'd messed everything up forever this time.

He was milliseconds from seeing a red card.

But it was yellow.

The ref held the yellow card up for everyone to see. Then he blew his whistle for half-time: *FWEE FWEEEEE*.

As Seth trudged off the pitch, Sam was being helped onto his feet by Brooke and Curtis. Seth could feel the other Freaks' eyes, burning him like lasers.

'We're s'posed to be mates,' moaned Sam.

'Yeah,' Seth told him. '*S'posed* to be.' Seth grabbed a water bottle from the side of the pitch and kept on walking. He didn't even stop when his dad called after him.

THE KING OF THE JUNGLE

Seth stood at the chain-link fence that ran around the five-a-side pitches. He didn't want to leave altogether, but he still wanted to be as far away from everyone else as he could get. He stared out at the green playing fields and thought about where it all started – when Mr Steele didn't pick him for the school team. 'Too slow,' that's what Steele had said. 'If I were you, I'd give up football. Have a go at something else. Dancing... or knitting.' Seth could still hear the words now. Maybe the miserable old goat was right. Maybe he should've just given up. He was sure he wouldn't be feeling as rubbish as he was now if he *had* taken up knitting. Knitting didn't make you petulant and crazy either. For the first time, he wished he'd never started Freaks United at all.

Then he felt a hand on his shoulder. It was his dad. 'What was all that about?' he asked.

'That tackle on Sam, that's not like you.'

'Maybe it is,' said Seth, sadly.

'I don't think so, mate. What's the matter?'

'I just couldn't take it. Seeing them laughing at us, making jokes, winding us up.'

'I don't think it was like that,' said Steve.

'Doesn't matter anyway,' Seth told him. 'There's no way we're winning this. They're way better.'

'It doesn't matter, though, does it?' asked Steve. 'Like it didn't matter when we played the school. Some of my mates'd kill me for saying this, but it *is* just a game.'

'It does matter, though,' Seth told him. 'It matters to me.'

'That much ,though? Hurting Sam like that?'

Seth turned away, stared out at the field. 'You don't get it.'

'You're right,' said Steve. 'Didn't realise how important this was to you.'

'It's not this.'

'Then what is it?' asked Steve.

'Doesn't matter,' Seth told him.

'Just tell me, I want to know.'

'All I want... all I've ever really wanted... is to be footballer.'

'I know, mate,' said Steve. 'I know how much you love your footie.'

'No. I mean a *real* footballer. A professional.'

'Right,' said Steve. 'OK.'

'And I wanted to win,' Seth told him. 'At first I thought that if we won the tournament, and got to meet Jesse Walters, he might've been able to get me a trial or something.'

Steve didn't say anything this time. The dark lines in his forehead just became deeper.

'But I think it's more than that,' said Seth. 'If I really want to be a footballer, it's not just about this tournament, it's about everything. I *have* to be a winner.'

'I get that,' said Steve.

'And all I really am...' Seth paused a moment. It was hard for him to say the next bit out loud. 'All I really am... is a loser.'

'That's not true. Don't say that.'

'It's so true,' said Seth. 'And that's why I lost it out there, went in on Sam like that. Because I'm not good enough and it hurts. It *actually* hurts.'

'Hey, come here.' Steve held his arms open for Seth and Seth didn't care who might be watching, or what anyone might think. He just hugged his dad. Alan Block was right. Hugs were the best.

'I'm so proud of you, son,' said Steve. 'Everything you've done, everything you've achieved. This whole thing, none of it would've happened if it wasn't for you. I know your mum would be proud of you too.'

Seth didn't say anything. He didn't think he'd be able to get the words around the massive lump in his throat.

'And while I don't know what you'd have to do to be a professional footballer,' Steve told him. 'I do know that if you set your mind to things, you make them happen.'

'Aww,' said a mocking voice from nearby. 'Isn't this touching?'

Mr Steele and Mr Cotton were standing there. Mr Steele had this evil sneer on his face and Mr Cotton shot him an angry frown.

'Sorry for... erm... interrupting,' said Mr Cotton.

'I'm not,' snapped Steele. 'I'm sorry for nothing.'

'What d'you want?' asked Steve.

'It's going quite badly for you both, isn't it?' mocked Steele.

Steve narrowed his eyes on the bald PE teacher. 'I asked you, what d'you want?'

'I just wanted to savour the moment,' Steele told him. 'Bask in my glory.'

'Lesley,' said Leon. 'Do we really need to do this?'

'It's Steele,' snapped Steele. 'And *yes*, we really need to do this. Y'see this pair, they've caused me quite the bit of bother.'

'You beat *us*,' said Steve. 'You got five hundred quid outta me!'

'You think I care about money?' asked Steele.

Steve shrugged. He obviously didn't know what Steele cared about. Seth didn't imagine Steele cared about much. Torturing defenceless kittens maybe?

'Well, it's nice and all,' Steele told him. 'But that's not what gets me out of bed in the morning.'

'So what does, then?' asked Steve. 'Let's hear it.'

'Revenge,' said Steele. 'Y'see, after the whole debacle with you and your lad, there were a few complaints. "You need to change your ways", they told me. "You need to be nice to the kids. More modern."'

'Well, you should be nice to the kids,' said Mr Cotton.

'Did I ask for your input?' snapped Steele before continuing. 'So, I've been playing along, pretending to be all nicey-nicey, all warm and fuzzy. Making everyone believe I'd taken it on board – all their nonsense. But it's like they say, a leopard never changes his spots. And d'you know what I am?'

'I've got a few suggestions,' said Steve. 'But there's kids knocking about.'

'I'm a leopard,' Steele told him. 'A jungle cat. The king of the jungle.'

'I think that's a lion,' said Steve.

'Not in my jungle,' snapped Mr Steele.

Mr Cotton cocked an eyebrow and stared at Seth, as if to say, 'What is this guy on?' Even in spite of everything Seth was feeling, he couldn't stop himself from smiling.

'No one makes a mug out of a leopard,' Steele told him. 'No one makes a mug out of Mr Steele. And you thought you had, didn't you? You and your Freaks. You thought you'd made a mug out of me. Well I'll tell you something, shall I?'

'I think you're going to anyway, aren't you,' said Steve, sarcastically.

'If anyone's making mugs out of anyone, it's me. I'm the mug-maker!'

Mr Cotton frowned. 'So what, you make mugs?'

'Not literally,' snapped Steele. 'Not literal mugs you drink out of. Idiots. Mugs as in idiots.'

'Oh right,' said Mr Cotton, and he smiled at Seth, letting him know he was having a little laugh at Steele's expense himself.

'You thought you could poach my best player?'

asked Steele. 'You thought you could steal young Daniel and there'd be no consequences? You were wrong. Doesn't work like that. Did you not wonder why things weren't going quite to plan? How I knew about the tournament ? Where your shirts went?'

Seth's jaw tightened. He knew Steele had been up to something.

'You're not the only one who likes a bit of spying,' Steele said to Seth.

'So what are you saying exactly?' asked Steve.

'What I'm saying, *exactly*, is that you might think young Daniel's a *Freak*, or whatever it is you call yourselves. But he's not. He's one of mine. One of MINE!'

Seth could feel fuses and gaskets blowing all over again. They never stood a chance with that pouty-mouthed snake Logan involved. Seth knew he should never have let him become a Freak. He should never have listened to Angelo and Beefy.

'Wow,' said Mr Cotton. 'That's pretty messed up.'

'But in a good way,' replied Steele. 'It was a good plan.'

'Not really in a good way,' Mr Cotton told him. 'So this whole thing you've just done, this whole speech – it's like the end of a James Bond film when the villain reveals his master plan to Bond, right before he sets the laser off to cut him in two.'

'I hadn't really thought about it like that,' said Steele. 'But why not?'

'So you're a Bond villain?' asked Mr Cotton. 'Is that what you're saying?'

'I'm not the villain here,' spat Steele. 'These pair, they're the villains!'

'So you used a spy to infiltrate their team,' said Mr Cotton.

'Hmm-mm.'

'You stole their shirts,' Mr Cotton went on.

'Well, not me personally.'

'And you brought a team here – and me,' said Mr Cotton, 'to sabotage their football team – who by the way, I think are great – to basically destroy everything they've worked really hard to build?'

'In a fashion.'

'And you're not the villain?' asked Mr Cotton.

Mr Steele could see there was no way out of this, so he didn't say anything else.

'Nice work,' said Mr Cotton. 'You've upset a group of twelve-year-old friends. Impressive.'

Mr Steele still didn't say anything. He just gave a little growl.

'I suggest you walk away right now,' said

Steve. 'Right. Now.'

Mr Steele stared at Steve, at the hulking size of the man. He swallowed. Then he just turned around and marched away, back over to the pitch.

'Wow,' said Mr Cotton again. 'Sorry, I didn't know about any of this. Has he always been that messed up? I mean, I'd heard a few stories.'

Seth nodded. 'Always.'

THE GAME'S UP

With the second-half about to start, Steve rounded up his team.

'What was all that about?' Logan asked Seth, nervously. 'With Steele?'

'I don't wanna cause a big hoo-ha,' said Steve. 'But I want to know if what that crackpot just told me was true. Dan...'

Logan stared at Steve. His eyes were wide, and he was poking his tongue into the side of his cheek. 'Yeah?'

'Have you been helping him?' asked Steve. 'Trying to wreck this tournament for us?'

Logan didn't say anything, which pretty much confirmed everything Mr Steele had told them. He stared at Steve for a few seconds and then down at the floor.

'What?' asked Angelo. 'He's a traitor?' He looked to Seth for an answer and Seth just popped his bottom lip over his top, doing his best to keep his mouth shut. He'd already caused enough trouble.

'Is that true?' asked Laura, hands on hips. 'You've been trying to mess things up?'

There was a long, long moment when no one said anything. All you could hear was the hubbub of the other kids and adults.

Then Logan confessed: 'I didn't want to. He made me.'

The others gasped as Laura shook her head. 'I can't believe this. You little snake.'

'Hold on a minute,' Steve told her. 'We don't know all the facts. What happened?'

'He came to see me,' Logan told them. 'Not long after I joined Freaks. He told me he'd get me a trial with United if I helped him out.'

Steve rubbed his face, like he didn't understand any of what was happening. 'This is crazy.'

'So it was you that nicked our shirts?' asked Angelo.

Logan stared at the fake green grass below him. 'Yeah.'

'So there weren't any ghosts?' asked Alan Block, sounding absolutely gutted.

'It was me,' Logan admitted.

'And you told him about the tournament?' asked Beefy.

'Yeah,' Logan whispered again. 'Everything – all me.'

'Told you it wasn't me,' said Alan Block.

Angelo put his arm around Alan's shoulder. 'I never thought it was.'

'Honestly?' asked Alan.

'Not my Alan,' said Angelo, and Seth rolled his eyes.

'I proper messed up,' Logan told them. 'I just really wanted a trial.'

Seth thought about what he'd just heard. He unfolded his arms and thought about what he'd done to get to this tournament – how he'd kept it from half the team. That had been pretty bad. And that was all about some stupid idea he might get a trial at United. When he really thought about it, he wasn't sure what he'd have done, had he been in Logan's shoes.

'I'll just call my mum,' said Logan. 'Get her to come and pick me up.'

Seth suddenly felt the urge to say something, stand up for Logan. Because the truth was, he was just as bad. 'You don't have to do that,' said Seth.

'I don't?' asked Logan, sounding surprised.

'He doesn't?' asked Angelo.

'What he did was messed up,' Seth told them. But this is *my* fault. If I hadn't wanted to come to this stupid tournament in the first place, none of this would've happened. I went behind everyone's backs. I'm just as bad. All this was ever meant to be was fun – us lot playing football, doing something we loved. And look at us. Fighting, kicking off, going behind each other's backs. This isn't fun.'

Alan Block shook his head. 'It's not,' he said, sombrely.

'So what do we do, then?' asked Beefy. 'Do we try and beat the other Freaks or not?'

FREAKS REUNITED

Just before the match was about to kick off, Seth led his team of Ninjas over to the other Freaks. 'Any chance we can have a word?'

'What's up?' asked Sam.

'Just, well...' Seth tried to get his words out, but he was nervous and embarrassed. 'Just with everything...'

But before he could finish, Mr Steele stormed over. 'What's going on?' he demanded to know.

'Nothing to do with you,' said Angelo.

'Nothing to do with me?' asked Mr Steele. 'Nothing to do with me!' he repeated, like it was the most absurd thing he'd ever heard.

Steve and Mr Cotton rushed over too, to see what all the fuss was about.

'Let's just leave the guys to it,' said Mr Cotton. 'You've done enough damage already.'

'I haven't done anywhere near enough damage,' Steele told him. 'The damage hasn't even begun!'

'You better walk away now,' said Steve.

'Or what?' asked Steele.

Steve glanced around, then leaned in close to Steele. He whispered something in the PE teacher's ear. Seth couldn't hear what his dad had said, but he saw the look on Mr Steele's face. He saw the red drain from his round cheeks. He saw his mouth close and turn down at the sides.

'Fine,' said Mr Steele. 'The damage *is* already done anyhow.' Then he cackled as he walked away, like some lame pantomime villain.

'What was all that about?' asked Curtis.

'It's Mr Steele,' said Seth. 'What d'you expect?'

'He reckons he's turned over a new leaf,' said Ryo.

'No way has he,' Seth told him. 'All this, he just wanted to destroy us – destroy Freaks United. This was his whole plan all along.'

'Really?' asked Alex, sounding surprised. 'I thought he'd genuinely changed.'

'A leopard never changes its spots,' said Seth. 'And he seems to think he's a leopard.'

Alan Block laughed at this. 'He's not a leopard.'

'He thinks he is,' Seth replied. 'You should've heard him going on about being king of the jungle and all that – he's so weird. Anyway...'

'It's true,' Logan cut in. 'He got me to spy for him. Made me tell him about the tournament. He even got me to steal Seth and everyone's shirts.'

Curtis pushed his glasses back against the bridge of his nose. 'You stole their shirts?'

'Yeah,' replied Logan. 'I'm the worst, I know. I'm so sorry, to everyone here. I was just thinking about myself.' Logan looked like a shell of himself. But Seth thought he was showing some class. He could've done a runner. That was what everyone would have expected Logan to do. But he was still here, explaining and apologising. Everyone stared at Logan and there were a few smiles and nods. No one had to say a word.

'I like your new shirts,' said Alex. 'Ninjas FC.'

'Cool name, right?' asked Angelo.

'Not bad,' said Curtis. 'Not bad at all.'

Angelo grinned, pleased that the name he'd come up was finally getting the recognition it deserved.

'But it wasn't Mr Steele's idea for you lot to come to this tournament was it?' asked John, towering above everyone. 'Not in the first place.'

Seth went quiet a moment, building up his courage. If Logan could apologise, Seth could definitely say sorry too. 'No,' said Seth. 'It was my idea.'

'And mine,' added Angelo.

'Mine too,' said Beefy.

'Mine three,' added Alan.

'It wasn't Alan's idea,' Seth told them. 'Ignore him.'

Alan Block just grinned.

'It was *my* fault,' said Seth. 'I should never have left you guys behind, I was a complete numpty.'

Curtis nodded. John 'hmm-mm'ed' and Sam just said, 'Yep.'

'So if you don't wanna play for Freaks again, I understand.'

'But *we* are Freaks United,' said Sam.

'Right,' replied Seth. 'I get it, you want me out. No worries...'

'No, Seth,' said Sam. 'We as in all of us. We're *all* Freaks United.'

A smile appeared on Seth's face. 'For real?'

'We're mates, aren't we?'

'Yeah, but...'

'Mates stick together,' Sam told him.

'But I didn't stick with you guys,' said Seth.

'And you're saying sorry, aren't you?' asked Sam.

'Yeah... and about going for you too. That was bang out of order.'

'I *was* winding you up a bit,' said Sam.

'Even so.'

'Excuse me,' interrupted the ref. 'Any chance we can get this match going?'

'In a minute, please,' Seth told him. 'This is important.'

'This is a cup final,' said the ref. 'Is it more important than a cup final?'

Seth stared at the ref for a long moment. Then he nodded firmly. 'It is,' said Seth. 'This is more important than anything.' He turned back to Sam and the other Freaks. He carried on as the ref just stood there, arms folded, looking around like he didn't have a clue what was happening. 'I knew you were winding me up,' said Seth, smiling.

'You deserved it,' Sam told him. 'As if you wouldn't have done the same thing, other way around?'

Seth thought about it. Sam made a good point. 'True.'

'We just wanted to be involved,' Sam told him. 'I'm not gonna lie, we were gutted when we found out out we'd been left out. You should've seen Alex.'

'I felt very hurt indeed,' said Alex. 'There were tears in my eyes. Tears of genuine sorrow.'

Seth did his best to smile at the friendly, well-spoken Goth. 'Sorry.'

'The whole point of Freaks,' said Sam, 'was not leaving people out, wasn't it?'

'But Steele, though?' asked Laura.

'Yeah,' said Seth. 'Steele?'

'Yeah,' agreed Sam. 'That was a mistake.'

'A mistake?' asked Seth. 'You sold your soul to the devil.'

Curtis looked over to check Steele was out of earshot. 'I think he might actually be the devil as well. Or a servant of Satan at the very least.'

'Cool,' said Alan Block.

The ref coughed, really loudly. 'Are we done, then?' he asked. 'This little *tête-à-tête* finished?'

'Potato-what?' asked Angelo.

'This little... this little conversation,' said the ref, growing more and more agitated.

Angelo looked at Seth, shook his head. 'Why not just say that, then?'

Beefy lifted his right shoulder and up and let it drop. He made his 'I dunno' sound.

'Are we ready?' asked the ref.

'Dunno,' said Curtis. 'What do we do now?'

Seth thought about it a moment. Then a big smile filled his face. 'Let's have some fun, Freaks United style!'

'Hallelujah!' cried Alan Block, his hands pressed together like he was praying. 'They're finally speaking my language! Hands in...'

Everyone put their hands in. No arguments.

'On the count of three,' said Alan. 'One... Two...' Seth looked over at Angelo and Beefy and grinned. The pair of them grinned back.

'THREE!' yelled Alan.

They all cheered, 'FREAKS UNITED!' together.

'I could cry, I'm so happy,' Alan Block told them.

A FREAKY FINAL

The ref finally got to blow his whistle and the second half kicked off. It was the most fun Seth could remember having in a long time. There were goals galore. Tricks, flicks, everything. No one was taking it seriously, and both sides were delighted whenever anyone scored. And pretty much everyone was on the scoresheet. Curtis curled one in. Logan launched a rocket. And Brooke bagged a back-heel. When Seth got his hat-trick, he looked over and saw his dad and Mr Cotton both clapping. The smile on Seth's face was colossal.

Mr Steele on the other-hand was jumping up and down, flapping his arms around angrily, like he was a bald red-faced bird and he was trying to take off. The sight and the thought of Steele as a bald bird, pushed Seth's smile even higher up his face.

When Alan Block banged one in, it all went

off. Both teams got together and did their customary line dance – hands on hips, kicking out their feet. The crowd were properly amused – and probably quite bemused too – by the whole thing. But the Freaks didn't care, they all just piled on top of Alan. He was like the mascot of the team – everyone's little brother. And they all loved him. When he got up, Alan and Angelo performed this whole elaborate handshake they must've been practising in secret for ages. There were lots of hand slaps, a few foot taps, a dollop of dabbing and a little bit of bum wiggling. Seth was amazed. Where had that come from? The pair could barely do a high-five the last time he'd checked.

When the ref blew the final whistle – *FWEEE FWEE-FWEE-FWEE* – the game had finished twelve–ten to the other Freaks. It didn't matter. All the Freaks were together and they all had their arms around one another, bobbing up and down, singing, '*Championes, Championes, Olé! Olé! Olé!*' like the United players did whenever they won a trophy. It wasn't quite what Seth had imagined at the start of the trip. In fact, it was the total opposite. But it was so much better!

And Steele's reaction was *even* better. He was losing it on the sideline, going ballistic, complaining that everyone was celebrating together. 'IT SHOULDN'T BE ALLOWED!' he shouted. 'IT'S UNNATURAL!' This was meant to be the culmination of his master plan – the total and utter destruction of Freaks United. But all he'd really seemed to do was bring the whole team closer together.

All was forgiven. All was forgotten. Aside from the having fun part. That was far from being forgotten. That would never be forgotten again as far as Seth was concerned. It was the best feeling ever, celebrating with his mates. And while his team hadn't won the game or the tournament, they'd had a blast. And Seth had remembered. This was what it was all about. *This*, right here. Having a laugh with your mates. Being a part of something. What was better than that?

Seth made a mental note to write down the Freaks United rules when he got the chance. In case he ever forgot again in the future. That way he could look at the rules and remember this moment. Remember how happy he was. While they would take some proper thinking about, he was pretty sure the rules would go something like this:

1. *Freaks United do not care about winning or losing.*

FREAKS UNITED – OFFSIDE!

2. *Freaks United play football because they love it.*

3. *Freaks United should always be fun (except when Big Steve makes you do warm-ups).*

4. *No Freak is any better than any other Freak.*

5. *No Freak gets left out.*

Seth could already imagine the team meeting when the rules would be debated. He was pretty certain some of the other Freaks would have some rules of their own. Alan would probably want everyone to go 'hands in' before every match. Angelo would want them to change their names to Ninjas FC. Beefy would probably want them to add 'Sicker' to their club badge. Even though they were just in his head, Seth was sure they were going to be an awesome set of rules.

Seth's thoughts were interrupted by Steele racing onto the pitch and trying to pull the group of kids apart. 'YOU'RE NOT MEANT TO BE FRIENDS!' he yelled. 'YOU'RE MEANT TO BE MORTAL ENEMIES!'

Seth and the others pushed Steele away, but he kept coming back, trying to pull them away from one another and stop them having fun. It didn't matter, no one was paying any attention.

Then the ref blew his whistle really, really loudly – *FWEEEEEEEEEE*! He held his red card aloft, waving it in Steele's face. 'YOU'RE OFF!' he shouted.

Two burly security guards grabbed Mr Steele and dragged his bald butt away. He was literally kicking and screaming, banging on about how 'football wasn't what it used to be' and how they were all 'namby-pamby ninny babies!'

FREAKS FOREVER

That evening, Seth, his dad and the rest of
Ninjas FC were enjoying fish and chips in a
restaurant overlooking the sea. The smell of
salt and vinegar filled Seth's nose and the bangs
and clangs from the kitchen filled his ears.
Everyone was smiling as they stuffed chips into
their mouths. Everyone was happy and excited,
talking about the match. Things were back to
the way they were before. The way they should
always have been. OK, Seth hadn't got to meet
his hero, Jesse Walters, or earned himself a
trial at United, but he'd realised some things
were more important – such as having fun with
your friends. Seth didn't want to give up on his
dream. No way. But he didn't want to go after
the things he wanted, only to be left miserable
and friendless either.

'Are you bummed out you didn't get to meet
Walters?' Angelo asked Seth.

'A bit. Not that much.'

'Me neither,' said Beefy and he stuffed a chunk of fish into his mouth. 'I'm happy.'

'You're mouth's full, Beefs,' Seth told him. 'Course you're happy.'

'Nothing wrong with liking your food.'

The three of them laughed and Seth was so glad to have his mates back. Mr Cotton had been right – what was the point of victory if you didn't have anyone to celebrate with? This was way better than winning the tournament, meeting Jesse Walters and everyone forcing smiles and pretending to be friends.

'No way,' said Angelo.

'No way what?' asked Seth.

No one answered. They were all silent and staring at Seth. Seth felt immediately uncomfortable. Why was everyone looking at him like that, like he was an alien or something?

Steve flicked his head at Seth and widened his eyes. Seth just stared back, confused. He shrugged.

'Behind you,' whispered Steve.

Seth frowned, realising it wasn't him everyone was gawping at. When he turned around, he also realised it wasn't just his dad and mates who were gawping. Everyone in the restaurant was. With good reason too.

Stood there – right there in the same place where Seth and his mates were eating fish and chips and slurping cola – was Jesse Walters.

The Jesse Walters. Sam and Alex and the others were with him.

'Woah,' said Seth. He felt even more nervous than he did before the five-a-side final. His heart was thumping even faster: *BADUMP-BADUMP-BADUMP.*

Jesse Walters was wearing his United tracksuit, the really cool one Seth wanted. His hair was dyed yellow with dark stripes – tiger-print style. He always had these insane haircuts. On most people, it would look ridiculous. But Walters was so cool, he could pull it off. He looked much shorter in real life than Seth imagined he would. But he had this massive presence, like a proper superstar. When he walked into a room, people noticed. He headed over to their table, led by Mr Cotton and the other Freaks.

'What's wrong with his head?' asked a familiar, cartoony voice. 'D'you think it's something bad?'

Seth spun round to come face-to-face with Shlumpy, Alan's red monkey puppet.

'What the...? When did you...?' He couldn't believe Alan had brought the puppet all this way.

Shlumpy lifted an arm to wave, 'Hiya, Se—'

But before it could finish, Seth had wrestled the puppet back under the table out of the sight of Jesse Walters – just in time.

'So, these are the rest of your team?' asked Jesse Walters. He smiled at Seth and the others with the brightest whitest teeth. The team grinned back, nervously, hoping the United player hadn't spotted Shlumpy.

Mr Cotton nodded. 'This is them. Is it OK if we join you?'

'Yeah,' replied Steve. 'Course it is. Sit yourselves down.'

Everyone pulled up chairs and gathered around. The whole thing was so amazing, even Beefy stopped stuffing his face for like a full five seconds.

Jesse Walters smiled at them all. 'These guys were telling me all about your team. Sounds like a right laugh.'

'It is,' replied Alan Block. 'Most of the time. But sometimes Seth won't let us put our hands in or make jokes.'

'Which one of you's Seth?' asked the footballer.

A red-faced Seth held his hand up. Not very high though. Only for a moment, just near his cheek. He suspected he was about to get a right telling off. From his all-time hero as well. He wondered what the other Freaks had said.

Whether they'd told Jesse Walters about what he'd done, how he'd left them out.

'You started the whole thing, yeah?' asked Jesse Walters. 'Freaks United and that?'

That wasn't what Seth had been expecting. 'Um, yeah.'

Jesse Walters held his fist out. 'My guy right here.'

Seth stared at it a moment, before Angelo nudged him. 'Bump him, then.'

Seth jolted into life. 'Ahh, yeah.' He bumped Jesse Walter's fist, feeling a bit self-conscious and awkward.

'Good work, man,' Jesse Walters said. 'See this is what I'm talking about – this boy's got initiative.'

'It wasn't just me,' Seth told him. He pointed to Angelo and Beefy. 'Ange and Beefy were there all the way.'

'Cool,' said Jesse, with a nod. He held his fist out to Beefy and Angelo too now, who both bumped it with no self-consciousness or awkwardness. 'Good to have mates you can count on, innit?'

Seth looked around at everyone and nodded. 'Yeah, it is. The best.'

'Come down to the training ground,' said Jesse Walters. 'If you all fancy it? Have a chat with the lads and that, I bet they'd love to hear about your team.'

'You reckon?' asked Seth, sounding a bit more high-pitched than he wanted.

'All day. As long as that's OK with your coaches.' He gave Steve and Mr Cotton a look.

'Sounds good to me,' said Steve.

'What 'bout you, Leon?' asked Jesse Walters. 'What you saying?'

'I'm the PE teacher,' Mr Cotton told him. 'Not the coach.'

'But you could be,' said Seth. 'Couldn't he, Dad? If he wanted?'

'Hey, the more, the merrier, for me.'

'OK,' said Mr Cotton. 'I'd be up for that!'

Seth beamed at Angelo and Beefy. This was just getting better and better.

Once Jesse Walters had signed autographs and shirts for all the Freaks – and everyone else in the restaurant – an expensive-looking car picked him up and drove him away.

Seth still couldn't get his head around it. Everything that had happened these past few days was squirming and wriggling about in his brain. He couldn't keep a hold of it all. 'All's well that ends well,' that's what his dad said. Today had most definitely ended well.

And it seemed like the day might end even

better for Steve. Seth suddenly realised his dad wasn't next to him. He was sitting at the corner of the table and was chatting away with Julie, Steele's trendy red-haired wife. Seth nudged Angelo and Beefy, and the three of them listened into the conversation.

'Sorry about everything that happened,' said Steve. 'With your fella.'

'My fella?' asked Julie.

'The PE teacher – Mr Steele?'

'He's not my fella,' Julie told him. She pulled a horrified face, like the suggestion was one of the most disgusting things she'd ever heard. 'Who told you that?'

Steve frowned as he thought it through, then he looked over at Alan Block, who was licking ice cream from his spoon. He noticed Steve looking at him and gave him a big grin. 'No one. I just assumed, I suppose.'

'Well you know what they say about assuming,' said Julie. 'I'm Alex's mum. I just came along to help out.'

Alex looked up. 'Did someone say my name?'

'Don't worry,' Julie told him. 'We're just talking about you.'

'OK, cool,' said Alex, then he got back to his in-depth video game conversation with Curtis.

'Psst,' whispered Seth. 'Alex.'

'Yeah?' said Alex, looking up.

'Is that your mum?' asked Seth.

'Yeah,' replied Alex.

'She doesn't look like your mum,' said Angelo.

'Doesn't she?'

'She's all bright and colourful,' said Beefy. 'And you're all... well... not.'

Alex shrugged. He didn't seem to mind.

'Is she single?' asked Seth.

Alex made this 'hmmm' sound as he thought. Then he nodded. 'Yeah, why?'

'No reason.'

'You thinking what I'm thinking?' asked Angelo.

'Dunno,' said Seth, unsure what Angelo was ever thinking.

'We get them together... Steve and Alex's mum?'

Seth looked over, saw the massive smile on his dad's face as he chatted away to Julie. She didn't even looked bored either. Seth smiled too, and for once Angelo and him were thinking the same thing. But before he could advance their plan any further, the sound of a spoon being clinked on an ice-cream sundae glass got everyone's attention.

Sam stood up from the table. 'Is it OK if I say a few words?'

'Go for it,' Steve told him.

'Me and some of the guys have been talking,' said Sam. 'And we're all happy everything's back to normal – Freaks United and all that...'

Everyone cheered.

'But there is one thing,' said Sam. 'We'd like Seth to do something for us, y'know, to make it all up.'

Seth blinked, confused. 'Me? What d'you want me to do?'

Sam smirked. 'I think you know what we want you to do.'

The following Wednesday the Freaks met up over on Barrowby field for their training session. The only difference was that Seth wasn't there first. Everyone was chatting, stretching, getting themselves ready for Steve's infamous 'warm-up', but Seth was nowhere to be seen.

'HERE HE IS!' shouted Tall John.

Seth trudged across the field towards them, hands in his pockets. Then he pulled the woolly donkey mask over his face.

As soon as the others saw him, they were in fits of laughter. And then came the donkey noises: 'EEYORE!', 'HEE-HAW!' Alan Block was once again making his chomping noise, grabbing clumps of grass from the ground and stuffing them into his mouth.

'Ha ha,' said Seth. 'You're all hilarious.'

'Give us a little spin then,' Sam told him.

Seth smiled to himself as turned around, showing off the plastic bum sewn into the back of his shorts.

'What a lovely little bum,' said Alan Block, in this strange voice that made him sound like an old farmer, and everyone laughed all over again.

'D'you want a donkey ride?' asked Seth.

'Me?' asked Alan, filled with excitement.

Seth got down on his hands and knees, and Alan bounded over. He climbed onto Seth's back and smacked the plastic backside. 'Giddyup, donkey! Giddyup!'

Angelo and Beefy were laughing so hard they were crying. Tall John was rolling around on the floor, he thought it was so funny.

Seth eeyored as he gave Alan Block a donkey ride around the field. The others howled with laughter.

If anyone else had been watching, they would definitely have thought this lot were a bunch of freaks.

And that's exactly what they were.

ABOUT THE AUTHOR

John Hickman is an award-winning screen-writer, director and author, based in Newcastle upon Tyne. John trained as a social worker, before completing an MA in Creative Writing at Newcastle University.

In addition to his books for children, John also writes for a number of television series, including *EastEnders* for BBC One, and *The Dumping Ground* for CBBC. His children's television script, *The Things*, was a winner of the BAFTA Rocliffe New Writing Competition, and his first book, *Freaks United*, was shortlisted for the 2017 James Reckitt Hull Children's Book Award.

A NOTE FROM JOHN

I really hope you enjoyed *Freaks United: Offside!*
How about sharing it with your friends? If you're
not already a member of a book club, why not
join, or even start one? Book clubs can be great
fun, and they give you a chance to talk about all
the things you did (or didn't!) like about a book.

Here are a few suggestions of what to think
about to get you going. (Of course, you don't have
to be in a book club – you can just do it for fun!)

The book's title...
- What did you think about this book when you
  first saw it?
- What did the team motto 'Fatter, Slower,
  Worser' make you think about the team?
- If you were to start your own football team,
  what would it be called and what would its
  motto be?

The book's characters...
- Who do you think is the funniest character
  and why?

- Would you like Seth as a friend? Why/why not?
- Did your view about any of the characters change by the end of the book?

Seth made some tough decisions at the start of the book.
- Do you think Seth was right or wrong not to tell the whole team about the tournament? Why/why not?
- What was it that made Seth put the tournament above his team?
- Have you ever been left out of something? Or have you been in Seth's position, and left people out? How did it make you feel?

Mr Cotton is very different to Mr Steele.
- What did Mr Steele do to try to show he'd changed his ways?
- Why do the boys like Mr Cotton so much?
- Mr Cotton is good at motivating the team. What motivates you to do your best? Do you motivate others?

Do you think it was right that things turned out the way they did?
- What did you think would happen at the end of the story? Were you right?

- Was the book only about football, or were other things as, or more, important?
- Did you feel sorry for Seth? Why/why not?
- Do you have a dream? Have you thought about ways that you might achieve it?

Would you recommend *Freaks United: Offside!* to other readers?
- Did you think *Freaks United: Offside!* was funny?
- Which part made you laugh the most?
- What do you think might happen with the Freaks next?

FREAKS UNITED

ISBN 978-1-78270-194-1

Seth, Beefy and Angelo can't believe it
when they aren't selected for the football
team at their new school. And things only
get worse when they are labelled the 'freaks'
who didn't make it. Do they give up on their
dreams, or do they find a way to show coach
Steele and his squad that they're wrong?

And so FREAKS UNITED is born –
and the team plans to live up to its name!
A fun footballing story about the kids
who don't get picked.

'If you don't know your left foot from
your right – and even if you do – *Freaks
United* is a book you'll love. It's great!'
Bali Rai